BEYOND THE DOORS OF DEATH

Beyond the
Doors of Death

ROBERT SILVERBERG
& DAMIEN BRODERICK

an imprint of

Rockville, Maryland

ISBN: 978-1-61242-112-4

www.PhoenixPick.com
Great Science Fiction & Fantasy
Free Ebook Every Month

Published by Phoenix Pick
an imprint of Arc Manor
P. O. Box 10339
Rockville, MD 20849-0339
www.ArcManor.com

PART ONE:

BORN
WITH THE
DEAD

ROBERT
SILVERBERG

BORN WITH THE DEAD:

INTRODUCTION

by Robert Silverberg

For most of its half-century-plus of existence the magazine that is formally known as *The Magazine of Fantasy and Science Fiction* but is more usually called *F&SF* has been a bastion of civilized and cultivated writing. That was true under its founding editors, Anthony Boucher and J. Francis McComas, and under such succeeding editors as Robert P. Mills and Avram Davidson. By the 1970s, editorial control had passed into the hands of Edward L. Ferman, who also happened to be the publisher of the magazine, and who functioned in admirable fashion in both capacities for many years thereafter.

My fiction had been appearing on and off in *F&SF* since the days of the Boucher-McComas administration; but it was Ed Ferman who turned me into a steady contributor. He published a flock of my short stories in the magazine in the 1960s, of which the best known was the much-anthologized "Sundance," and then, as I began to turn away from shorter fiction in favor of novellas and novels, Ferman let me know that he would be interested in publishing some of my longer work also.

In December, 1972, just after the publication of my novel *Dying Inside*, I got a note from Ferman that mentioned that he had just received a review copy of that book. "I simply wanted to tell you what a fine and moving and painful experience it was to read it," he wrote, going on to compare the novel favorably to recent works by Bernard Malamud and Chaim Potok. And he added in a postscript, "The editor in me has just popped up, and I can't help asking what I have to do to see your next novel. If it's anything near the quality of *Dying Inside*, I'll go higher than our top rate."

I wasn't planning to write another novel just then—1972 was a particularly turbulent year for me, involving, among other things, the reverberations involved in my recent transplantation from New York to California, and I was unwilling to commit myself to any very lengthy work until things had settled down a little in my life. And I was already working on a longish short story called "Trips" for an anthology Ferman was editing in collaboration with Barry Malzberg. But I did tell him that I had another long story in mind to write after that, one that would probably run to novella length, and it was his if he wanted it. Ferman replied at once that he did, and early in April of 1973 wrote me to say, "I don't recall if I've mentioned length, but with the added pages I can take as much as 30,000 words. I don't expect that long a story, but if it develops that way I'd be happy to have it."

The story was "Born With the Dead," and it did develop that way.

It had the feel of a major story from the moment I conceived it. I had played with the idea of the resuscitation of the dead in fiction since my 1957 novel *Recalled to Life*, and now, I felt, I was ready to return to it with a kind of culminating statement on the subject. I let Ferman know that I was already at work on it, and that it was going to be a big one. To which he replied on April 16, 1973 that he proposed to make the story the centerpiece of a special Robert Silverberg issue of the magazine.

That had real impact on me. Over the years *F&SF* had done a handful of special issues honoring its favorite contributors—Theodore Sturgeon, Ray Bradbury, Fritz Leiber, Poul Anderson, James Blish, and one or two others. Each special issue featured a portrait of the writer on the cover, a major new story by him, several critical essays, and a bibliography. All of the writers chosen had been favorites of mine since my days as an avid adolescent reader; and now, suddenly, in my mid-thirties and just reaching the peak of my career, I found myself chosen to join their company. It gave me a nice shiver down the spine.

But of course I had to write a story *worthy* of that company—and this at a time when my private life was in chaos and the world about me, there in the apocalyptic days of the late Nixon era, was pretty chaotic too. So every day's work was an ordeal. The ease and fervor with which I had written so many stories and novels just a few years ago had left me now, never to return. Sometimes I managed no more than a couple of paragraphs in an entire morning; sometimes, even less. The weeks dragged by; I entered the second month of the project with more than half the story still to tell. (By way of comparison: *Dying Inside*, also a difficult thing to write and three times as long, took me just nine weeks.) And now it was the middle of May; I had begun the story in late March. But somehow, finally, I regained my stride in early June, and the closing scenes, grim as their content was, were much easier to write than those that had gone before. One night in early June I was at the movies—Marlon Brando's *Last Tango in Paris*, it was—when the closing paragraphs of the story began to form in my mind. I turned to my wife and asked her for the notebook she always carried, and began to scribble sentences in the dark during the final minutes of the film. The movie ended; the lights came on; the theater emptied; and there I sat, still writing. "Are you a movie critic?" an usher asked me. I shook my head and went on writing.

So the thing was done, and I knew that I had hooked me a big fish. The next day I typed out what I had written in the theater, and set about preparing a final draft for Ed Ferman, and on June 16, 1973 I sent it to him with a note that said, "Here It Is. I feel exhausted, drained, relieved, pleased, proud, etc. I hope the thing is worthy of all the sweat that went into it. What I'm going to do tomorrow is don my backpack and head for the Sierra for a week in the back country at 10,000 feet, a kind of rite of purification after all these months of crazy intense typing."

"I could not be more pleased with 'Born With the Dead,'" Ferman replied four days later. (E-mail was mere science fiction in those days.) "It seems to me that it brings to a peak the kind of thing you've been doing with *Book of Skulls* and *Dying Inside*." (I had not noticed until that moment the string of death-images running through the titles of those three practically consecutive works of mine.) "I don't think there is a wrong move in this story, and it comes together beautifully in the ending, which I found perfect and quite moving."

The story appeared in the April, 1974 *F&SF*, which was indeed the special Robert Silverberg issue, with an Ed Emshwiller portrait of me on the cover in my best long-haired 1970s psychedelic mode, and essays about me within by Barry Malzberg and Tom Clareson, along with a Silverberg bibliography in very small type (so it didn't fill half the issue). "Born With the Dead" went on to win the Nebula award in 1975 and the Locus award as well, and finished a close second in the Hugo voting. Since then it has been reprinted in innumerable anthologies, translated into a dozen foreign languages, and several times has been optioned for motion picture production.

And now it comes around once more, in a startlingly new guise. The original story is still here. But now the splendid Australian-born writer Damien Broderick has taken it as the starting point for a brilliant new novella that carries the afterlife adventures of Jorge Klein far into the future, a novella that widens and widens to an almost Stapledonian conceptual breadth; and, along the way, Broderick has also taken a second look at some of the unwritten implications of my own story, filling in elements of the background that I did not pause to explore. It pleases me very much that my story of forty years ago has given rise to such a dazzling new companion.

I said above that "the original story is still here," and so it is, but I also point out that it is a story of forty years ago. "Oh, sir, things change," says one of the characters in "Born with the Dead" at the end of the third chapter; and indeed they do. Time marches along and even the most visionary of science fiction gets out of date. The science fiction of Olaf Stapledon (1886-1950) is supreme in our field for its soaring vision of the billions of years to come, as his great novels *Last and First Men* and *Star Maker* demonstrate, but even he, though he could tell us all about the dizzyingly far future, got almost everything wrong at shorter range. Writing in 1930, Stapledon completely failed to foresee the rise of Adolf Hitler just three years later, and spoke of the Germany of his day as "the most pacific [of nations], a stronghold of enlightenment." Instead he singled out Mussolini, who was already in power, as the strongest figure in Europe ("a man whose genius in action combined with his rhetoric and crudity of thought to make him a very successful dictator"). Most—not all—of Stapledon's portrait of the world of the late twentieth and early twenty-first century is equally wrongheaded—"awkward and naive," as Gregory Benford said in his introduction to a 1988 edition of the book, and even "ludicrous," as Brian Aldiss once observed. Stapledon's account of the near future was so far off the mark that in a 1953 American edition of *Last and First Men* the publisher simply deleted most of the first three chapters of the sixteen-chapter book.

I did not intend "Born with the Dead" as a work of prophecy—I never seriously believed that by 1993, when the story takes place, a process would exist by which the dead could be brought back to life. I was writing a parable, a strange love story, a speculative view of a new kind of society that could arise provided one big assumption (that of the possibility of rekindling the dead) were granted, but not any sort of literal prediction. And time has left the story behind to the extent that 1993 did not see any such rebirth process as I depict. So I have made two small emendations in the original text. It takes place in 2033, now, instead of 1993, so that readers who are new to the story will not find themselves stumbling over what seems to them an annoying anachronism. And at one point a character boards a plane belonging to an airline that was long out of business by the time the 1993 of my story arrived; I have changed the airline's name to something more contemporary. Otherwise the text is as I wrote it in 1973.

I have rarely had as much difficulty writing a story as I had with this one; but all that hard work lies decades behind me, the story is still here, and I am delighted to see it returning to print now accompanied by Damien Broderick's extraordinary expansion and extension of my original concept.

—Robert Silverberg

One

And what the dead had no speech for, when living,
They can tell you, being dead: the communication
Of the dead is tongued with fire beyond the language
    of the living.

                      T.S. Eliot: *Little Gidding*

Supposedly his late wife Sybille was on her way to Zanzibar. That was what they told him, and he believed it. Jorge Klein was at that stage in his search when he would believe anything, if belief would only lead him to Sybille. Anyway, it wasn't so absurd that she would go to Zanzibar. Sybille had always wanted to go there. In some unfathomable obsessive way the place had seized the center of her consciousness long ago. When she was alive it hadn't been possible for her to go there, but now, loosed from all bonds, she would be drawn toward Zanzibar like a bird to its nest, like Ulysses to Ithaca, like a moth to a flame.

The plane, a small Air Zanzibar Staniford ST-912, took off more than half empty from Dar es Salaam at 0915 on a mild bright morning, gaily circled above the dense masses of mango trees, red-flowering flamboyants, and tall coconut palms along the aquamarine shores of the Indian Ocean, and headed northward on the short hop across the strait to Zanzibar. This day—Wednesday, the ninth of March, 2033—would be an unusual one for Zanzibar: five deads were aboard the plane, the first of their kind ever to visit that fragrant isle. Daud Mahmoud Barwani, the health officer on duty that morning at Zanzibar's Karume Airport, had been warned of this by the emigration

15

officials on the mainland. He had no idea how he was going to han-
dle the situation, and he was apprehensive: these were tense times in
Zanzibar. Times are always tense in Zanzibar. Should he refuse them
entry? Did deads pose any threat to Zanzibar's ever-precarious political stability? What about subtler menaces? Deads might be carriers
of dangerous spiritual maladies. Was there anything in the Revised
Administrative Code about refusing visas on grounds of suspected
contagions of the spirit? Daud Mahmoud Barwani nibbled moodily
at his breakfast—a cold chapatti, a mound of cold curried potato—
and waited without eagerness for the arrival of the deads.

Almost two and a half years had passed since Jorge Klein had last
seen Sybille: the afternoon of Monday, October 14, 2030, the day of
her funeral. That day she lay in her casket as though merely asleep,
her beauty altogether unmarred by her final ordeal: pale skin, dark
lustrous hair, delicate nostrils, full lips. Iridescent gold and violet fab-
ric enfolded her serene body; a shimmering electrostatic haze, faintly
perfumed with a jasmine fragrance, protected her from decay. For
five hours she floated on the dais while the rites of parting were read
and the condolences were offered—offered almost furtively, as if her
death were a thing too monstrous to acknowledge with a show of
strong feeling; then, when only a few people remained, the inner core
of their circle of friends, Klein kissed her lightly on the lips and sur-
rendered her to the silent dark-clad men whom the Cold Town had
sent. She had asked in her will to be rekindled; they took her away in
a black van to work their magic on her corpse. The casket, retreating
on their broad shoulders, seemed to Klein to be disappearing into
a throbbing gray vortex that he was helpless to penetrate. Presumably he would never hear from her again. In those days the deads
kept strictly to themselves, sequestered behind the walls of their self-
imposed ghettos; it was rare ever to see one outside the Cold Towns,
rare even for one of them to make oblique contact with the world of
the living.

So a redefinition of their relationship was forced on him. For nine
years it had been Jorge and Sybille, Sybille and Jorge, I and thou
forming *we*, above all *we*, a transcendental *we*. He had loved her with
almost painful intensity. In life they had gone everywhere together,

16

had done everything together, shared research tasks and classroom assignments, thought interchangeable thoughts, expressed tastes that were nearly always identical, so completely had each permeated the other. She was a part of him, he of her, and until the moment of her unexpected death he had assumed it would be like that forever. They were still young, he thirty-eight, she thirty-four, decades to look forward to. Then she was gone. And now they were mere anonymities to one another, she not Sybille but only a dead, he not Jorge but only a warm. She was somewhere on the North American continent, walking about, talking, eating, reading, and yet she was gone, lost to him, and it behooved him to accept that alteration in his life, and outwardly he did accept it, but yet, though he knew he could never again have things as they once had been, he allowed himself the indulgence of a lingering wistful hope of regaining her.

Shortly the plane was in view, dark against the brightness of the sky, a suspended mote, an irritating fleck in Barwani's eye, growing larger, causing him to blink and sneeze. Barwani was not ready for it. When Ameri Kombo, the flight controller in the cubicle next door, phoned him with the routine announcement of the landing, Barwani replied, "Notify the pilot that no one is to debark until I have given clearance. I must consult the regulations. There is possibly a peril to public health." For twenty minutes he let the plane sit, all hatches sealed, on the quiet runway. Wandering goats emerged from the shrubbery and inspected it. Barwani consulted no regulations. He finished his modest meal; then he folded his arms and sought to attain the proper state of tranquility. These deads, he told himself, could do no harm. They were people like all other people, except that they had undergone extraordinary medical treatment. He must overcome his superstitious fear of them: he was no peasant, no silly clovepicker, nor was Zanzibar an abode of primitives. He would admit them, he would give them their anti-malaria tablets as though they were ordinary tourists, he would send them on their way. Very well. Now he was ready. He phoned Ameri Kombo. "There is no danger," he said. "The passengers may exit."

There were nine altogether, a sparse load. The four warms emerged first, looking somber and a little congealed, like people who had had to travel with a party of uncaged cobras. Barwani knew them all: the German consul's wife, the merchant Chowdhary's son, and two Chinese engineers, all returning from brief holidays in Dar. He waved them through the gate without formalities. Then came the deads, after an interval of half a minute: probably they had been sitting together at one end of the nearly empty plane and the others had been at the other. There were two women, three men, all of them tall and surprisingly robust-looking. He had expected them to shamble, to shuffle, to limp, to falter, but they moved with aggressive strides, as if they were in better health now than when they had been alive. When they reached the gate, Barwani stepped forward to greet them, saying softly, "health regulations, come this way, kindly." They were breathing, undoubtedly breathing: he tasted an emanation of liquor from the big red-haired man, a mysterious and pleasant sweet flavor, perhaps anise, from the dark-haired woman. It seemed to Barwani that their skins had an odd waxy texture, an unreal glossiness, but possibly that was his imagination; white skins had always looked artificial to him. The only certain difference he could detect about the deads was in their eyes, a way they had of remaining unnervingly fixed in a single intense gaze for many seconds before shifting. Those were the eyes, Barwani thought, of people who had looked upon the Emptiness without having been swallowed into it. A turbulence of questions erupted within him: What is it like, how do you feel, what do you remember, where did you go? He left them unspoken. Politely he said, "Welcome to the isle of cloves. We ask you to observe that malaria has been wholly eradicated here through extensive precautionary measures, and to prevent recurrence of unwanted disease we require of you that you take these tablets before proceeding further." Tourists often objected to that; these people swallowed their pills without a word of protest. Again Barwani yearned to reach toward them, to achieve some sort of contact that might perhaps help him to transcend the leaden weight of being. But an aura, a shield of strangeness, surrounded these five, and though he was an amiable man who tended to fall into conversations easily with strangers, he passed them on in silence to Mponda the immigration man.

Mponda's high forehead was shiny with sweat, and he chewed at his lower lip; evidently he was as disturbed by the deads as Barwani.

He fumbled forms, he stamped a visa in the wrong place, he stammered while telling the deads that he must keep their passports overnight. "I shall post them by messenger to your hotel in the morning," Mponda promised them, and sent the visitors onward to the baggage pickup area with undue haste.

Klein had only one friend with whom he dared talk about it, a colleague of his at UCLA, a sleek supple Parsee sociologist from Bombay named Framji Jijibhoi, who was as deep into the elaborate new subculture of the deads as a warm could get. "How can I accept this?" Klein demanded. "I can't accept it at all. She's out there somewhere, she's alive, she's—"

Jijibhoi cut him off with a quick flick of his fingertips. "No, dear friend," he said sadly, "not alive, not alive at all, merely rekindled. You must learn to grasp the distinction."

Klein could not learn to grasp the distinction. Klein could not learn to grasp anything having to do with Sybille's death. He could not bear to think that she had passed into another existence from which he was totally excluded. To find her, to speak with her, to participate in her experience of death and whatever lay beyond death, became his only purpose. He was inextricably bound to her, as though she were still his wife, as though Jorge-and-Sybille still existed in any way.

He waited for letters from her, but none came. After a few months he began trying to trace her, embarrassed by his own compulsiveness and by his increasingly open breaches of the etiquette of this sort of widowerhood. He traveled from one Cold Town to another—Sacramento, Boise, Ann Arbor, Louisville—but none would admit him, none would even answer his questions. Friends passed on rumors to him, that she was living among the deads of Tucson, of Roanoke, of Rochester, of San Diego, but nothing came of these tales; then Jijibhoi, who had tentacles into the world of the rekindled in many places, and who was aiding Klein in his quest even though he disapproved of its goal, brought him an authoritative-sounding report that she was at Zion Cold Town in southeastern Utah. They turned him away there too, but not entirely cruelly, for he did manage to secure plausible evidence that that was where Sybille really was.

19

In the summer of '32 Jijibhoi told him that Sybille had emerged from Cold Town seclusion. She had been seen, he said, in Newark, Ohio, touring the municipal golf course at Octagon State Memorial in the company of a swaggering red-haired archaeologist named Kent Zacharias, also a dead, formerly a specialist in the mound-building Hopewellian cultures of the Ohio Valley. "It is a new phase," said Jijibhoi, "not unanticipated. The deads are beginning to abandon their early philosophy of total separatism. We have started to observe them as tourists visiting our world—exploring the life-death interface, as they like to term it. It will be very interesting, dear friend." Klein flew at once to Ohio and without ever actually seeing her, tracked her from Newark to Chillicothe, from Chillicothe to Marietta, from Marietta into West Virginia, where he lost her trail somewhere between Moundsville and Wheeling. Two months later she was said to be in London, then in Cairo, then Addis Ababa. Early in '33 Klein learned, via the scholarly grapevine—an ex-Californian now at Nyerere University in Arusha—that Sybille was on safari in Tanzania and was planning to go, in a few weeks, across to Zanzibar.

Of course. For ten years she had been working on a doctoral thesis on the establishment of the Arab Sultanate in Zanzibar in the early nineteenth century—studies unavoidably interrupted by other academic chores, by love affairs, by marriage, by financial reverses, by illnesses, death, and other responsibilities—and she had never actually been able to visit the island that was so central to her. Now she was free of all entanglements. Why shouldn't she go to Zanzibar at last? Why not? Of course: she was heading for Zanzibar. And so Klein would go to Zanzibar too, to wait for her.

As the five disappeared into taxis, something occurred to Barwani. He asked Mponda for the passports and scrutinized the names. Such strange ones: Kent Zacharias, Nerita Tracy, Sybille Klein, Anthony Gracchus, Laurence Mortimer. He had never grown accustomed to the names of Europeans. Without the photographs he would be unable to tell which were the women, which the men. Zacharias, Tracy, Klein...ah. *Klein.* He checked a memo, two weeks old, tacked to his desk. Klein, yes. Barwani telephoned the Shirazi Hotel—a project that consumed several minutes—and asked to speak with the American who had arrived ten days before, that slender man whose lips had been pressed tight in tension, whose eyes had glittered with fatigue, the one who had asked a little service of Barwani, a special favor, and had dashed him a much-needed hundred shillings as payment in advance. There was a lengthy delay, no doubt while porters searched the hotel, looking in the men's room, the bar, the lounge, the garden, and then the American was on the line. "The person about whom you inquired has just arrived, sir," Barwani told him.

Two

The dance begins. Worms underneath fingertips, lips beginning
to pulse, heartache and throat-catch. All slightly out of step
and out of key, each its own tempo and rhythm. Slowly,
connections. Lip to lip, heart to heart, finding self in other,
dreadfully, tentatively, burning...notes finding themselves in
chords, chords in sequence, cacophony turning to polyphonous
contrapuntal chorus, a diapason of celebration.

R.D. Laing: *The Bird of Paradise*

Sybille stands timidly at the edge of the municipal golf course at
Octagon State Memorial in Newark, Ohio, holding her sandals in
her hand and surreptitiously working her toes into the lush, immacu-
late carpet of dense, close-cropped lime-green grass. It is a summer
afternoon in 2032, very hot; the air, beautifully translucent, has that
timeless midwestern shimmer, and the droplets of water from the
morning sprinkling have not yet burned off the lawn. Such extraordinary grass! She hadn't often seen grass like that in California, and
certainly not at Zion Cold Town in thirsty Utah. Kent Zacharias,
towering beside her, shakes his head sadly. "A golf course!" he mutters.
"One of the most important prehistoric sites in North America and
they make a golf course out of it! Well, I suppose it could have been
worse. They might have bulldozed the whole thing and turned it into
a municipal parking lot. Look, there, do you see the earthworks?"

She is trembling. This is her first extended journey outside the
Cold Town, her first venture into the world of the warms since her
rekindling, and she is picking up threatening vibrations from all the
life that burgeons about her. The park is surrounded by pleasant little

houses, well kept. Children on bicycles rocket through the streets. In front of her, golfers are merrily slamming away. Little yellow golf carts clamber with lunatic energy over the rises and dips of the course. There are platoons of tourists who, like herself and Zacharias, have come to see the Indian mounds. There are dogs running free. All this seems menacing to her. Even the vegetation—the thick grass, the manicured shrubs, the heavy-leafed trees with low-hanging boughs—disturbs her. Nor is the nearness of Zacharias reassuring, for he too seems inflamed with undeadlike vitality; his face is florid, his gestures are broad and overanimated, as he points out the low flat-topped mounds, the grassy bumps and ridges making up the giant joined circle and octagon of the ancient monument. Of course, these mounds are the mainspring of his being, even now, five years post mortem. Ohio is his Zanzibar.

"—once covered four square miles. A grand ceremonial center, the Hopewellian equivalent of Chichén Itzá, of Luxor, of—" He pauses. Awareness of her distress has finally filtered through the intensity of his archaeological zeal. "How are you doing?" he asks gently.

She smiles a brave smile. Moistens her lips. Inclines her head toward the golfers, toward the tourists, toward the row of darling little houses outside the rim of the park. Shudders.

"Too cheery for you, is it?"

"Much," she says.

Cheery. Yes. A cheery little town, a magazine-cover town, a chamber-of-commerce town. Newark lies becalmed on the breast of the sea of time: but for the look of the automobiles, this could be 1990 or 1970 or perhaps 1940. Yes. Motherhood, baseball, apple pie, church every Sunday. Yes. Zacharias nods and makes one of the signs of comfort at her. "Come," he whispers. "Let's go toward the heart of the complex. We'll lose the twenty-first century along the way."

With brutal imperial strides he plunges into the golf course. Long-legged Sybille must work hard to keep up with him. In a moment they are within the embankment, they have entered the sacred octagon, they have penetrated the vault of the past, and at once Sybille feels they have achieved a successful crossing of the interface between life and death. How still it is here! She senses the powerful presence of the forces of death, and those dark spirits heal her unease. The encroachments of the world of the living on these precincts of the dead become insignificant: the houses outside the park are no longer in view, the golfers are mere foolish incorporeal shadows, the bustling yellow golf carts become beetles, the wandering tourists are invisible.

She is overwhelmed by the size and symmetry of the ancient site. What spirits sleep here? Zacharias conjures them, waving his hands like a magician. She has heard so much from him already about these people, these Hopewellians—What did they call themselves? How can we ever know?—who heaped up these ramparts of earth two millennia ago. Now he brings them to life for her with gestures and low urgent words. He whispers fiercely:

—Do you see them?

And she does see them. Mists descend. The mounds reawaken; the mound-builders appear. Tall, slender, swarthy, nearly naked, clad in shining copper breastplates, in necklaces of flint disks, in bangles of bone and mica and tortoise shell, in heavy chains of bright lumpy pearls, in rings of stone and terra cotta, in armlets of bears' teeth and panthers' teeth, in spool-shaped metal ear-ornaments, in furry loincloths. Here are priests in intricately woven robes and awesome masks. Here are chieftains with crowns of copper rods, moving in frosty dignity along the long earthen-walled avenue. The eyes of these people glow with energy. What an enormously vital, enormously profligate culture they sustain here! Yet Sybille is not alienated by their throbbing vigor, for it is the vigor of the dead, the vitality of the vanished.

Look, now. Their painted faces, their unblinking gazes. This is a funeral procession. The Indians have come to these intricate geometrical enclosures to perform their acts of worship, and now, solemnly parading along the perimeters of the circle and the octagon, they pass onward, toward the mortuary zone beyond. Zacharias and Sybille are left alone in the middle of the field. He murmurs to her:

—Come. We'll follow them.

He makes it real for her. Through his cunning craft she has access to this community of the dead. How easily she has drifted backward across time! She learns here that she can affix herself to the sealed past at any point; it's only the present, open-ended and unpredictable, that is troublesome. She and Zacharias float through the misty

24

meadow, no sensation of feet touching ground; leaving the octagon, they travel now down a long grassy causeway to the place of the burial mounds, at the edge of a dark forest of wide-crowned oaks. They enter a vast clearing. In the center the ground has been plastered with clay, then covered lightly with sand and fine gravel; on this base the mortuary house, a roofless four-sided structure with walls consisting of rows of wooden palisades, has been erected. Within this is a low clay platform topped by a rectangular tomb of log cribbing, in which two bodies can be seen: a young man, a young woman, side by side, bodies fully extended, beautiful even in death. They wear copper breastplates, copper ear-ornaments, copper bracelets, necklaces of gleaming yellowish bears' teeth.

Four priests station themselves at the corners of the mortuary house. Their faces are covered by grotesque wooden masks topped by great antlers, and they carry wands two feet long, effigies of the death-cup mushroom in wood sheathed with copper. One priest commences a harsh, percussive chant. All four lift their wands and abruptly bring them down. It is a signal; the depositing of grave-goods begins. Lines of mourners bowed under heavy sacks approach the mortuary house. They are unweeping, even joyful, faces ecstatic, eyes shining, for these people know what later cultures will forget, that death is no termination but rather a natural continuation of life. Their departed friends are to be envied. They are honored with lavish gifts, so that they may live like royalty in the next world: out of the sacs come nuggets of copper, meteoric iron, and silver, thousands of pearls, shell beads, beads of copper and iron, buttons of wood and stone, heaps of metal ear-spools, chunks and chips of obsidian, animal effigies carved from slate and bone and tortoise shell, ceremonial copper axes and knives, scrolls cut from mica, human jawbones inlaid with turquoise, dark coarse pottery, needles of bone, sheets of woven cloth, coiled serpents fashioned from dark stone, a torrent of offerings, heaped up around and even upon the two bodies.

At length the tomb is choked with gifts. Again there is a signal from the priests. They elevate their wands and the mourners, drawing back to the borders of the clearing, form a circle and begin to sing a somber, throbbing funeral hymn. Zacharias, after a moment, sings with them, wordlessly embellishing the melody with heavy melismas. His voice is a rich *basso cantante,* so unexpectedly beautiful that Sybille is moved almost to confusion by it, and looks at him in awe. Abruptly he breaks off, turns to her, touches her arm, leans down to say:

—You sing too.

Sybille nods hesitantly. She joins the song, falteringly at first, her throat constricted by self-consciousness; then she finds herself becoming part of the rite, somehow, and her tone becomes more confident. Her high clear soprano soars brilliantly above the other voices.

Now another kind of offering is made: boys cover the mortuary house with heaps of kindling—twigs, dead branches, thick boughs, all sorts of combustible debris—until it is quite hidden from sight, and the priests cry a halt. Then, from the forest, comes a woman bearing a blazing firebrand, a girl, actually, entirely naked, her sleek fair-skinned body painted with bizarre horizontal stripes of red and green on breasts and buttocks and thighs, her long glossy black hair flowing like a cape behind her as she runs. Up to the mortuary house she sprints; breathlessly she touches the firebrand to the kindling, here, here, here, performing a wild dance as she goes, and hurls the torch into the center of the pyre. Skyward leap the flames in a ferocious rush. Sybille feels seared by the blast of heat. Swiftly the house and tomb are consumed.

While the embers still glow, the bringing of earth gets under way. Except for the priests, who remain rigid at the cardinal points of the site, and the girl who wielded the torch, who lies like discarded clothing at the edge of the clearing, the whole community takes part. There is an open pit behind a screen of nearby trees; the worshipers, forming lines, go to it and scoop up soil, carrying it to the burned mortuary house in baskets, in buckskin aprons, in big moist clods held in their bare hands. Silently they dump their burdens on the ashes and go back for more.

Sybille glances at Zacharias; he nods; they join the line. She goes down into the pit, gouges a lump of moist black clayey soil from its side, takes it to the growing mound. Back for another, back for another. The mound rises rapidly, two feet above ground level now, three, four, a swelling circular blister, its outlines governed by the unchanging positions of the four priests, its tapering contours formed by the tamping of scores of bare feet. Yes, Sybille thinks, this is a valid way of celebrating death, this is a fitting rite. Sweat runs down her body, her clothes become stained and muddy, and still she runs to the earth-quarry, runs from there to the mound, runs to the quarry, runs to the mound, runs, runs, transfigured, ecstatic.

Then the spell breaks. Something goes wrong, she does not know what, and the mists clear, the sun dazzles her eyes, the priests and the mound-builders and the unfinished mound disappear. She and Zacharias are once again in the octagon, golf carts roaring past them on every side. Three children and their parents stand just a few feet from her, staring, staring, and a boy about ten years old points to Sybille and says in a voice that reverberates through half of Ohio, "Dad, what's wrong with those people? Why do they look so weird?"

Mother gasps and cries, "*Quiet*, Tommy, don't you have any manners?" Dad, looking furious, gives the boy a stinging blow across the face with the tips of his fingers, seizes him by the wrist, tugs him toward the other side of the park, the whole family following in their wake.

Sybille shivers convulsively. She turns away, clasping her hands to her betraying eyes. Zacharias embraces her. "It's all right," he says tenderly. "The boy didn't know any better. It's all right."

"Take me away from here!"

"I want to show you—"

"Some other time. Take me away. To the motel. I don't want to see anything. I don't want anybody to see me."

He takes her to the motel. For an hour she lies face down on the bed, racked by dry sobs. Several times she tells Zacharias she is unready for this tour, she wants to go back to the Cold Town, but he says nothing, simply strokes the tense muscles of her back, and after a while the mood passes. She turns to him and their eyes meet and he touches her and they make love in the fashion of the deads.

Three

Newness is renewal: *ad hoc enim venit, ut renovemur in illo*; making it new again, as on the first day; *herrlich wie am ersten Tag.* Reformation, or renaissance; rebirth. Life is Phoenix-like, always being born again out of its own death. The true nature of life is resurrection; all life is life after death, a second life, reincarnation. *Totus hic ordo revolubilis testatio est resurrectionis mortuorum.* The universal pattern of recurrence bears witness to the resurrection of the dead.

Norman O. Brown: *Love's Body*

"The rains shall be commencing shortly, gentleman and lady," the taxi driver said, speeding along the narrow highway to Zanzibar Town. He had been chattering steadily, wholly unafraid of his passengers. He must not know what we are, Sybille decided. "Perhaps in a week or two they begin. These shall be the long rains. The short rains come in the last of November and December."

"Yes, I know," Sybille said.

"Ah, you have been to Zanzibar before?"

"In a sense," she replied. In a sense she had been to Zanzibar many times, and how calmly she was taking it, now that the true Zanzibar was beginning to superimpose itself on the template in her mind, on that dream-Zanzibar she had carried about so long! She took everything calmly now: nothing excited her, nothing aroused her. In her former life the delay at the airport would have driven her into a fury: a ten-minute flight, and then to be trapped on the runway twice as long! But she had remained tranquil throughout it all, sitting almost immobile, listening vaguely to what Zacharias was saying and

28

occasionally replying as if sending messages from some other planet. And now Zanzibar, so placidly accepted. In the old days she had felt a sort of paradoxical amazement whenever some landmark familiar from childhood geography lessons or the movies or travel posters—the Grand Canyon, the Manhattan skyline, Taos Pueblo—turned out in reality to look exactly as she imagined it would; but now here was Zanzibar, unfolding predictably and unsurprisingly before her, and she observed it with a camera's cool eye, unmoved, unresponsive.

The soft, steamy air was heavy with a burden of perfumes, not only the expected pungent scent of cloves but also creamier fragrances which perhaps were those of hibiscus, frangipani, jacaranda, penetrating the cab's open window like probing tendrils. The imminence of the long rains was a tangible pressure, a presence, a heaviness in the atmosphere: at any moment a curtain might be drawn aside and the torrents would start. The highway was lined by two shaggy green walls of palms broken by tin-roofed shacks; behind the palms were mysterious dark groves, dense and alien. Along the edge of the road was the usual tropical array of obstacles: chickens, goats, naked children, old women with shrunken, toothless faces, all wandering around untroubled by the taxi's encroachment on their right-of-way. On through the rolling flatlands the cab sped, out onto the peninsula on which Zanzibar Town sits. The temperature seemed to be rising perceptibly minute by minute; a fist of humid heat was clamping tight over the island. "Here is the waterfront, gentleman and lady," the driver said. His voice was an intrusive hoarse purr, patronizing, disturbing. The sand was glaringly white, the water a dazzling glassy blue; a couple of dhows moved sleepily across the mouth of the harbor, their lateen sails bellying slightly as the gentle sea breeze caught them. "On this side, please—" An enormous white wooden building, four stories high, a wedding cake of long verandahs and cast-iron railings, topped by a vast cupola. Sybille, recognizing it, anticipated the driver's spiel, hearing it like a subliminal pre-echo: "Beit al-Ajaib, the House of Wonders, former government house. Here the Sultan was often make great banquets, here the famous of all Africa came homaging. No longer in use. Next door the old Sultan's Palace, now Palace of People. You wish to go in House of Wonders? Is open: we stop, I take you now."

29

"Another time," Sybille said faintly. "We'll be here awhile."

"You not here just a day like most?"

"No, a week or more. I've come to study the history of your island. I'll surely visit the Beit al-Ajaib. But not today."

"Not today, no. Very well: you call me, I take you anywhere. I am Ibuni." He gave her a gallant toothy grin over his shoulder and swung the cab inland with a ferocious lurch, into the labyrinth of winding streets and narrow alleys that was Stonetown, the ancient Arab quarter.

All was silent here. The massive white stone buildings presented blank faces to the streets. The windows, mere slits, were shuttered. Most doors—the famous paneled doors of Stonetown, richly carved, studded with brass, cunningly inlaid, each door an ornate Islamic masterpiece—were closed and seemed to be locked. The shops looked shabby, and the small display windows were speckled with dust. Most of the signs were so faded Sybille could barely make them out:

PREMCHAND'S EMPORIUM
MONJI'S CURIOS
ABDULLAH'S BROTHERHOOD STORE
MOTILAL'S BAZAAR

The Arabs were long since gone from Zanzibar. So were most of the Indians, though they were said to be creeping back. Occasionally, as it pursued its intricate course through the maze of Stonetown, the taxi passed elongated black limousines, probably of Russian or Chinese make, chauffeur-driven, occupied by dignified self-contained dark-skinned men in white robes. Legislators, so she supposed them to be, en route to meetings of state. There were no other vehicles in sight, and no pedestrians except for a few women, robed entirely in black, hurrying on solitary errands. Stonetown had none of the vitality of the countryside; it was a place of ghosts, she thought, a fitting place for vacationing deads. She glanced at Zacharias, who nodded and smiled, a quick quirky smile that acknowledged her perception and told her that he too had had it. Communication was swift among the deads and the obvious rarely needed voicing.

The route to the hotel seemed extraordinarily involuted, and the driver halted frequently in front of shops, saying hopefully, "You want brass chests, copper pots, silver curios, gold chains from China?" Though Sybille gently declined his suggestions, he continued to point out bazaars and emporiums, offering earnest recommendations of quality and moderate price, and gradually she realized, getting her bearings in the town, that they had passed certain corners more than once. Of course: the driver must be in the pay of shopkeepers who hired him to lure tourists.

"Please take us to our hotel," Sybille said, and when he persisted in his huckstering—"Best ivory here, best lace"—she said it more firmly, but she kept her temper. Jorge would have been pleased by her transformation, she thought; he had all too often been the immediate victim of her fiery impatience. She did not know the specific cause of the change. Some metabolic side-effect of the rekindling process, maybe, or maybe her two years of communion with Guidefather at the Cold Town, or was it, perhaps, nothing more than the new knowledge that all of time was hers, that to let oneself feel hurried now was absurd?

"Your hotel is this," Ibuni said at last.

It was an old Arab mansion—high arches, innumerable balconies, musty air, electric fans turning sluggishly in the dark hallways. Sybille and Zacharias were given a sprawling suite on the third floor, overlooking a courtyard lush with palms, vermilion nandi, kapok trees, poinsettia, and agapanthus. Mortimer, Gracchus, and Nerita had long since arrived in the other cab and were in an identical suite one floor below. "I'll have a bath," Sybille told Zacharias. "Will you be in the bar?"

"Very likely. Or strolling in the garden."

He went out. Sybille quickly shed her travel-sweaty clothes. The bathroom was a Byzantine marvel, elaborate swirls of colored tile, an immense yellow tub standing high on bronze eagle-claw-and-globe legs. Lukewarm water dribbled in slowly when she turned the tap. She smiled at her reflection in the tall oval mirror. There had been a mirror somewhat like it at the rekindling house. On the morning after her awakening, five or six deads had come into her room to celebrate with her her successful transition across the interface, and they had had that big mirror with them; delicately, with great ceremoniousness, they had drawn the coverlet down to show herself to her in it, naked, slender, narrow-waisted, high-breasted, the beauty of her body unchanged, marred neither by dying nor by rekindling, indeed enhanced by it, so that she had become more youthful-looking and even radiant in her passage across that terrible gulf.

—You're a very beautiful woman.

That was Pablo. She would learn his name and all the other names later.

—I feel such a flood of relief. I was afraid I'd wake up and find myself a shriveled ruin.

—That could not have happened, Pablo said.

—And never will happen, said a young woman. Nerita, she was.

—But deads do age, don't they?

—Oh, yes, we age, just as the warms do. But not *just* as.

—More slowly?

—Very much more slowly. And differently. All our biological processes operate more slowly, except the functions of the brain, which tend to be quicker than they were in life.

—Quicker?

—You'll see.

—It all sounds ideal.

—We are extremely fortunate. Life has been kind to us. Our situation is, yes, ideal. We are the new aristocracy.

—The new aristocracy—

Sybille slipped slowly into the tub, leaning back against the cool porcelain, wriggling a little, letting the tepid water slide up as far as her throat. She closed her eyes and drifted peacefully. All of Zanzibar was waiting for her. *Streets I never thought I should visit.* Let Zanzibar wait. Let Zanzibar wait. *Words I never thought to speak. When I left my body on a distant shore.* Time for everything, everything in its due time.

—*You're a very beautiful woman,* Pablo had told her, not meaning to flatter.

Yes. She had wanted to explain to them, that first morning, that she didn't really care all that much about the appearance of her body,

32

that her real priorities lay elsewhere, were "higher," but there hadn't been any need to tell them that. They understood. They understood everything. Besides, she did care about her body. Being beautiful was less important to her than it was to those women for whom physical beauty was their only natural advantage, but her appearance mattered to her; her body pleased her and she knew it was pleasing to others, it gave her access to people, it was a means of making connections, and she had always been grateful for that. In her other existence her delight in her body had been flawed by the awareness of the inevitability of its slow steady decay, the certainty of the loss of that accidental power that beauty gave her, but now she had been granted exemption from that: she would change with time but she would not have to feel, as warms must feel, that she was gradually falling apart. Her rekindled body would not betray her by turning ugly. No.

—We are the new aristocracy—

After her bath she stood a few minutes by the open window, naked to the humid breeze. Sounds came to her: distant bells, the bright chatter of tropical birds, the voices of children singing in a language she could not identify. Zanzibar! Sultans and spices, Livingstone and Stanley, Tippu Tib the slaver, Sir Richard Burton spending a night in this very hotel room, perhaps. There was a dryness in her throat, a throbbing in her chest: a little excitement coming alive in her after all. She felt anticipation, even eagerness. All Zanzibar lay before her. Very well. Get moving, Sybille, put some clothes on, let's have lunch, a look at the town.

She took a light blouse and shorts from her suitcase. Just then Zacharias returned to the room, and she said, not looking up, "Kent, do you think it's all right for me to wear these shorts here? They're—" A glance at his face and her voice trailed off. "What's wrong?"

"I've just been talking to your husband."

"He's *here?*"

"He came up to me in the lobby. Knew my name. 'You're Zacharias,' he said, with a Bogarty little edge to his voice, like a deceived movie husband confronting the Other Man. 'Where is she? I have to see her.'"

"Oh, no, Kent."

33

"I asked him what he wanted with you. 'I'm her husband,' he said, and I told him, 'Maybe you were her husband once, but things have changed,' and then—"

"I can't imagine Jorge talking tough. He's such a *gentle* man, Kent! How did he look?"

"Schizoid," Zacharias said. "Glassy eyes, muscles bunching in his jaws, signs of terrific pressure all over him. He knows he's not supposed to do things like this, doesn't he?"

"Jorge knows exactly how he's supposed to behave. Oh, Kent, what a stupid mess! Where is he now?"

"Still downstairs. Nerita and Laurence are talking to him. You don't want to see him, do you?"

"Of course not."

"Write him a note to that effect and I'll take it down to him. Tell him to clear off."

Sybille shook her head. "I don't want to hurt him."

"Hurt him? He's followed you halfway around the world like a lovesick boy, he's tried to violate your privacy, he's disrupted an important trip, he's refused to abide by the conventions that govern the relationships of warms and deads, and you—"

"He loves me, Kent."

"He loved you. All right, I concede that. But the person he loved doesn't exist any more. He has to be made to realize that."

Sybille closed her eyes. "I don't want to hurt him. I don't want you to hurt him either."

"I won't hurt him. Are you going to see him?"

"No," she said. She grunted in annoyance and threw her shorts and blouse into a chair. There was a fierce pounding at her temples, a sensation of being challenged, of being threatened, that she had not felt since that awful day at the Newark mounds. She strode to the window and looked out, half expecting to see Jorge arguing with Nerita and Laurence in the courtyard. But there was no one down there except a houseboy who looked up as if her bare breasts were beacons and gave her a broad dazzling smile. Sybille turned her back to him and said dully, "Go back down. Tell him that it's impossible for me to see him. Use that word. Not that I *won't* see him, not that I *don't want to* see him, not that it isn't *right* for me to see him, just that it's impossible. And then phone the airport. I want to go back to Dar on the evening plane."

"But we've only just arrived!"

"No matter. We'll come back some other time. Jorge is very persistent; he won't accept anything but a brutal rebuff, and I can't do that to him. So we'll leave."

Klein had never seen deads at close range before. Cautiously, uneasily, he stole quick intense looks at Kent Zacharias as they sat side by side on rattan chairs among the potted palms in the lobby of the hotel. Jijibhoi had told him that it hardly showed, that you perceived it more subliminally than by any outward manifestation, and that was true; there was a certain look about the eyes, of course, the famous fixity of the deads, and there was something oddly pallid about Zacharias' skin *beneath* the florid complexion, but if Klein had not known what Zacharias was, he might not have guessed it. He tried to imagine this man, this red-haired red-faced dead archaeologist, this digger of dirt mounds, in bed with Sybille. Doing with her whatever it was that the deads did in their couplings. Even Jijibhoi wasn't sure. Something with hands, with eyes, with whispers and smiles, not at all genital—so Jijibhoi believed. *This is Sybille's lover I'm talking to. This is Sybille's lover.* How strange that it bothered him so. She had had affairs when she was living; so had he; so had everyone; it was the way of life. But he felt threatened, overwhelmed, defeated, by this walking corpse of a lover.

Klein said, "Impossible?"

"That was the word she used."

"Can't I have ten minutes with her?"

"Impossible."

"Would you let me see her for a few moments, at least? I'd just like to find out how she looks."

"Don't you find it humiliating, doing all this scratching around just for a glimpse of her?"

"Yes."

"And you still want it?"

"Yes."

Zacharias sighed. "There's nothing I can do for you. I'm sorry."

"Perhaps Sybille is tired from having done so much traveling. Do you think she might be in a more receptive mood tomorrow?"

"Maybe," Zacharias said. "Why don't you come back then?"

"You've been very kind."

"*De nada.*"

"Can I buy you a drink?"

"Thanks, no," Zacharias said. "I don't indulge any more. Not since—" He smiled.

Klein could smell whiskey on Zacharias' breath. All right, though. All right. He would go away. A driver waiting outside the hotel grounds poked his head out of his cab window and said hopefully, "Tour of the island, gentleman? See the clove plantations, see the athlete stadium?"

"I've seen them already," Klein said. He shrugged. "Take me to the beach."

He spent the afternoon watching turquoise wavelets lapping pink sand. The next morning he returned to Sybille's hotel, but they were gone, all five of them, gone on last night's flight to Dar, said the apologetic desk clerk. Klein asked if he could make a telephone call, and the clerk showed him an ancient instrument in an alcove near the bar. He phoned Barwani. "What's going on?" he demanded. "You told me they'd be staying at least a week!"

"Oh, sir, things change," Barwani said softly.

Four

What portends? What will the future bring? I do not know, I have no presentiment. When a spider hurls itself down from some fixed point, consistently with its nature, it always sees before it only an empty space wherein it can find no foothold however much it sprawls. And so it is with me: always before me an empty space; what drives me forward is a consistency which lies behind me. This life is topsy-turvy and terrible, not to be endured.

Soren Kierkegaard: Either/Or

Jijibhoi said, "In the entire question of death who is to say what is right, dear friend? When I was a boy in Bombay it was not unusual for our Hindu neighbors to practice the rite of suttee, that is, the burning of the widow on her husband's funeral pyre, and by what presumption may we call them barbarians? Of course"—his dark eyes flashed mischievously—"we did call them barbarians, though never when they might hear us. Will you have more curry?"

Klein repressed a sigh. He was getting full, and the curry was fiery stuff, of an incandescence far beyond his usual level of tolerance; but Jijibhoi's hospitality, unobtrusively insistent, had a certain hieratic quality about it that made Klein feel like a blasphemer whenever he refused anything in his home. He smiled and nodded, and Jijibhoi, rising, spooned a mound of rice into Klein's plate, buried it under curried lamb, bedecked it with chutneys and sambals. Silently, unbidden, Jijibhoi's wife went to the kitchen and returned with a cold bottle of Heineken. She gave Klein a shy grin as she set it down before him. They worked well together, these two Parsees, his hosts.

They were an elegant couple—striking, even. Jijibhoi was a tall, erect man with a forceful aquiline nose, dark Levantine skin, jet-black hair, a formidable mustache. His hands and feet were extraordinarily small; his manner was polite and reserved; he moved with a quickness of action bordering on nervousness. Klein guessed that he was in his early forties, though he suspected his estimate could easily be off by ten years in either direction. His wife—strangely, Klein had never been told her name—was younger than her husband, nearly as tall, fair of complexion—a light-olive tone—and voluptuous of figure. She dressed invariably in flowing silken saris; Jijibhoi affected western business dress, suits and ties in style twenty years out of date. Klein had never seen either of them bareheaded: she wore a kerchief of white linen, he a brocaded skullcap that might lead people to mistake him for an Oriental Jew. They were childless and self-sufficient, forming a closed dyad, a perfect unit, two segments of the same entity, conjoined and indivisible, as Klein and Sybille once had been. Their harmonious interplay of thought and gesture made them a trifle disconcerting, even intimidating, to others. As Klein and Sybille once had been.

Klein said, "Among your people—"

"Oh, very different, very different, quite unique. You know of our funeral custom?"

"Exposure of the dead, isn't it?"

Jijibhoi's wife giggled. "A very ancient recycling scheme!"

"The Towers of Silence," Jijibhoi said. He went to the dining room's vast window and stood with his back to Klein, staring out at the dazzling lights of Los Angeles. The Jijibhois' house, all redwood and glass, perched precariously on stilts near the crest of Benedict Canyon, just below Mulholland: the view took in everything from Hollywood to Santa Monica. "There are five of them in Bombay," said Jijibhoi, "on Malabar Hill, a rocky ridge overlooking the Arabian Sea. They are centuries old, each one circular, several hundred feet in circumference, surrounded by a stone wall twenty or thirty feet high. When a Parsee dies—do you know of this?"

"Not as much as I'd like to know."

"When a Parsee dies, he is carried to the Towers on an iron bier by professional corpse-bearers; the mourners follow in procession, two by two, joined hand to hand by holding a white handkerchief between them. A beautiful scene, dear Jorge. There is a doorway in the stone wall through which the corpse-bearers pass, carrying their burden. No one else may enter the Tower. Within is a circular platform paved with large stone slabs and divided into three rows of shallow, open receptacles. The outer row is used for the bodies of males, the next for those of females, the innermost one for children. The dead one is given a resting-place; vultures rise from the lofty palms in the gardens adjoining the Towers; within an hour or two, only bones remain. Later, the bare, sun-dried skeleton is cast into a pit at the center of the Tower. Rich and poor crumble together there into dust."

"And all Parsees are—ah—buried in this way?"

"Oh, no, no, by no means," Jijibhoi said heartily. "All ancient traditions are in disrepair nowadays, do you not know? Our younger people advocate cremation or even conventional interment. Still, many of us continue to see the beauty of our way."

"—beauty?—"

Jijibhoi's wife said in a quiet voice, "To bury the dead in the ground, in a moist tropical land where diseases are highly contagious, seems not sanitary to us. And to burn a body is to waste its substance. But to give the bodies of the dead to the efficient hungry birds—quickly, cleanly, without fuss—is to us a way of celebrating the economy of nature. To have one's bones mingle in the pit with the bones of the entire community is, to us, the ultimate democracy."

"And the vultures spread no contagions themselves, feeding as they do on the bodies of—"

"Never," said Jijibhoi firmly. "Nor do they contract our ills."

"And I gather that you both intend to have your bodies returned to Bombay when you—" Aghast, Klein paused, shook his head, coughed in embarrassment, forced a weak smile. "You see what this radioactive curry of yours has done to my manners? Forgive me. Here I sit, a guest at your dinner table, quizzing you about your funeral plans!"

Jijibhoi chuckled. "Death is not frightening to us, dear friend. It is—one hardly needs say it, does one?—it is a natural event. For a time we are here, and then we go. When our time ends, yes, she and I will give ourselves to the Towers of Silence."

His wife added sharply, "Better there than the Cold Towns! Much better!"

Klein had never observed such vehemence in her before.

Jijibhoi swung back from the window and glared at her. Klein had never seen that before either. It seemed as if the fragile web of elaborate courtesy that he and these two had been spinning all evening was suddenly unraveling, and that even the bonds between Jijibhoi and his wife were undergoing strain. Agitated now, fluttery, Jijibhoi began to collect the empty dishes, and after a long awkward moment said, "She did not mean to give offense."

"Why should I be offended?"

"A person you love chose to go to the Cold Towns. You might think there was implied criticism of her in my wife's expression of distaste for—"

Klein shrugged. "She's entitled to her feelings about rekindling. I wonder, though—"

He halted, uneasy, fearing to probe too deeply.

"Yes?"

"It was irrelevant."

"Please," Jijibhoi said. "We are old friends."

"I was wondering," said Klein slowly, "if it doesn't make things hard for you, spending all your time among deads, studying them, mastering their ways, devoting your whole career to them, when your wife evidently despises the Cold Towns and everything that goes on in them. If the theme of your work repels her, you must not be able to share it with her."

"Oh," Jijibhoi said, tension visibly going from him, "if it comes to that, I have even less liking for the entire rekindling phenomenon than she."

"You do?" This was a side of Jijibhoi that Klein had never suspected. "It repels you? Then why did you choose to make such an intensive survey of it?"

Jijibhoi looked genuinely amazed. "What? Are you saying one must have personal allegiance to the subject of one's field of scholarship?" He laughed. "You are of Jewish birth, I think, and yet your doctoral thesis was concerned, was it not, with the early phases of the Third Reich?"

40

Klein winced. "Touché!"

"I find the subculture of the deads irresistible, as a sociologist," Jijibhoi went on. "To have such a radical new aspect of human existence erupt during one's career is an incredible gift. There is no more fertile field for me to investigate. Yet I have no wish, none at all, ever to deliver myself up for rekindling. For me, my wife, it will be the Towers of Silence, the hot sun, the obliging vultures—and finis, the end, no more, terminus."

"I had no idea you felt this way. I suppose if I'd known more about Parsee theology, I might have realized—"

"You misunderstand. Our objections are not theological. It is that we share a wish, an idiosyncratic whim, not to continue beyond the allotted time. But also I have serious reservations about the impact of rekindling on our society. I feel a profound distress at the presence among us of these deads, I feel a purely private fear of these people and the culture they are creating, I feel even an abhorrence for—" Jijibhoi cut himself short. "Your pardon. That was perhaps too strong a word. You see how complex my attitudes are toward this subject, my mixture of fascination and repulsion? I exist in constant tension between those poles. But why do I tell you all this, which if it does not disturb you, must surely bore you? Let us hear about your journey to Zanzibar."

"What can I say? I went, I waited a couple of weeks for her to show up, I wasn't able to get near her at all, and I came home. All the way to Africa and I never even had a glimpse of her."

"What a frustration, dear Jorge!"

"She stayed in her hotel room. They wouldn't let me go upstairs to her."

"They?"

"Her entourage," Klein said. "She was traveling with four other deads, a woman and three men. Sharing her room with the archaeologist, Zacharias. He was the one who shielded her from me, and did it very cleverly, too. He acts as though he owns her. Perhaps he does. What can you tell me, Framji? Do the deads marry? Is Zacharias her new husband?"

"It is very doubtful. The terms 'wife' and 'husband' are not in use among the deads. They form relationships, yes, but pair-bonding

41

seems to be uncommon among them, possibly altogether unknown. Instead they tend to create supportive pseudo-familial groupings, of three or four or even more individuals, who—"

"Do you mean that all four of her companions in Zanzibar are her lovers?"

Jijibhoi gestured eloquently. "Who can say? If you mean in a physical sense, I doubt it, but one can never be sure. Zacharias seems to be her special companion, at any rate. Several of the others may be part of her pseudo-family also, or all, or none. I have reason to think that at certain times every dead may claim a familial relationship to all others of his kind. Who can say? We perceive the doings of these people, as they say, through a glass, darkly."

"I don't see Sybille even that well. I don't even know what she looks like now."

"She has lost none of her beauty."

"So you've told me before. But I want to see her myself. You can't really comprehend, Framji, how much I want to see her. The pain I feel, not able—"

"Would you like to see her right now?"

Klein shook in a convulsion of amazement. "What? What do you mean? Is she—"

"Hiding in the next room? No, no, nothing like that. But I do have a small surprise for you. Come into the library." Smiling expansively, Jijibhoi led the way from the dining room to the small study adjoining it, a room densely packed from floor to ceiling with books in an astonishing range of languages—not merely English, French, and German, but also Sanskrit, Hindi, Gujerati, Farsi, the tongues of Jijibhoi's polyglot upbringing among the tiny Parsee colony of Bombay, a community in which no language once cherished was ever discarded. Pushing aside a stack of dog-eared professional journals, he drew forth a glistening picture-cube, activated its inner light with a touch of his thumb, and handed it to Klein.

The sharp, dazzling holographic image showed three figures on a broad grassy plain that seemed to have no limits and was without trees, boulders, or other visual interruptions, an endlessly unrolling green carpet under a blank death-blue sky. Zacharias stood at the left, his face averted from the camera; he was looking down, tinkering

42

with the action of an enormous rifle. At the far right stood a stocky, powerful-looking dark-haired man whose pale, harsh-featured face seemed all beard and nostrils. Klein recognized him: Anthony Gracchus, one of the deads who had accompanied Sybille to Zanzibar. Sybille stood beside him, clad in khaki slacks and a crisp white blouse. Gracchus' arm was extended; evidently he had just pointed out a target to her, and she was intently aiming a gun nearly as big as Zacharias'.

Klein shifted the cube about, studying her face from various angles, and the sight of her made his fingers grow thick and clumsy, his eyelids to quiver. Jijibhoi had spoken truly: she had lost none of her beauty. Yet she was not at all the Sybille he had known. When he had last seen her, lying in her casket, she had seemed to be a flawless marble image of herself, and she had that same surreal statuary appearance now. Her face was an expressionless mask, calm, remote, aloof; her eyes were glossy mysteries; her lips registered a faint, enigmatic, barely perceptible smile. It frightened him to behold her this way, so alien, so unfamiliar. Perhaps it was the intensity of her concentration that gave her that forbidding marmoreal look, for she seemed to be pouring her entire being into the task of taking aim. By tilting the cube more extremely, Klein was able to see what she was aiming at: a strange awkward bird moving through the grass at the lower left, a bird larger than a turkey, round as a sack, with ash-gray plumage, a whitish breast and tail, yellow-white wings, and short, comical yellow legs. Its head was immense and its black bill ended in a great snubbed hook. The creature seemed solemn, rather dignified, and faintly absurd; it showed no awareness that its doom was upon it. How odd that Sybille should be about to kill it, she who had always detested the taking of life: Sybille the huntress now, Sybille the lunar goddess, Sybille-Diana!

Shaken, Klein looked up at Jijibhoi and said, "Where was this taken? On that safari in Tanzania, I suppose."

"Yes. In February. This man is the guide, the white hunter."

"I saw him in Zanzibar. Gracchus, his name is. He was one of the deads traveling with Sybille."

"He operates a hunting preserve not far from Kilimanjaro," Jijibhoi said, "that is set aside exclusively for the use of the deads. One of the more bizarre manifestations of their subculture, actually. They hunt only those animals which—"

Klein said impatiently, "How did you get this picture?"

"It was taken by Nerita Tracy, who is one of your wife's companions."

"I met her in Zanzibar too. But how—"

"A friend of hers is an acquaintance of mine, one of my informants, in fact, a valuable connection in my researches. Some months ago I asked him if he could obtain something like this for me. I did not tell him, of course, that I meant it for you." Jijibhoi looked close. "You seem troubled, dear friend."

Klein nodded. He shut his eyes as though to protect them from the glaring surfaces of Sybille's photograph. Eventually he said in a flat, toneless voice, "I have to get to see her."

"Perhaps it would be better for you if you would abandon—"

"*No.*"

"Is there no way I can convince you that it is dangerous for you to pursue your fantasy of—"

"No," Klein said. "Don't even try. It's necessary for me to reach her. Necessary."

"How will you accomplish this, then?"

Klein said mechanically, "By going to Zion Cold Town."

"You have already done that. They would not admit you."

"This time they will. They don't turn away deads."

The Parsee's eyes widened. "You will surrender your own life? Is this your plan? What are you saying, Jorge?"

Klein, laughing, said, "That isn't what I meant at all."

"I am bewildered."

"I intend to infiltrate. I'll disguise myself as one of them. I'll slip into the Cold Town the way an infidel slips into Mecca." He seized Jijibhoi's wrist. "Can you help me? Coach me in their ways, teach me their jargon?"

"They'll find you out instantly."

"Maybe not. Maybe I'll get to Sybille before they do."

"This is insanity," Jijibhoi said quietly.

"Nevertheless. You have the knowledge. Will you help me?"

Gently Jijibhoi withdrew his arm from Klein's grasp. He crossed the room and busied himself with an untidy bookshelf for some moments, fussily arranging and rearranging. At length he said, "There is little I can do for you myself. My knowledge is broad but not deep, not deep enough. But if you insist on going through with this, Jorge, I can introduce you to someone who may be able to assist you. He is one of my informants, a dead, a man who has rejected the authority of the Guidefathers, a person who is *of* the deads but not with them. Possibly he can instruct you in what you would need to know."

"Call him," Klein said.

"I must warn you he is unpredictable, turbulent, perhaps even treacherous. Ordinary human values are without meaning to him in his present state."

"Call him."

"If only I could discourage you from—"

"Call him."

Five

Quarreling brings trouble. These days lions roar a great deal. Joy follows grief. It is not good to beat children much. You had better go away now and go home. It is impossible to work today. You should go to school every day. It is not advisable to follow this path, there is water in the way. Never mind, I shall be able to pass. We had better go back quickly. These lamps use a lot of oil. There are no mosquitoes in Nairobi. There are no lions here. There are people here, looking for eggs. Is there water in the well? No, there is none. If there are only three people, work will be impossible today.

D.V. Perrott: *Teach Yourself Swahili*

Gracchus signals furiously to the porters and bellows, "*Shika njia hii hii!*" Three turn, two keep trudging along. "*Ninyi nyote!*" he calls. "*Fanga kama hivi!*" He shakes his head, spits, flicks sweat from his forehead. He adds, speaking in a lower voice and in English, taking care that they will not hear him, "Do as I say, you malevolent black bastards, or you'll be deader than I am before sunset!"

Sybille laughs nervously. "Do you always talk to them like that?"

"I try to be easy on them. But what good does it do, what good does any of it do? Come on, let's keep up with them."

It is less than an hour after dawn, but already the sun is very hot, here in the flat dry country between Kilimanjaro and Serengeti. Gracchus is leading the party northward across the high grass, following the spoor of what he thinks is a quagga, but breaking a trail in the high grass is hard work and the porters keep veering away toward a ravine that offers the tempting shade of a thicket of thorn trees, and he constantly has to harass them in order to hold them to the route he wants. Sybille has noticed that Gracchus shouts fiercely to his blacks, as if they were no more than recalcitrant beasts, and speaks of them behind their backs with a rough contempt, but it all seems done for show, all part of his white-hunter role: she has also noticed, at times when she was not supposed to notice, that privately Gracchus is in fact gentle, tender, even loving among the porters, teasing them—she supposes—with affectionate Swahili banter and playful mock-punches. The porters are role-players too: they behave in the traditional manner of their profession, alternately deferential and patronizing to the clients, alternately posing as all-knowing repositories of the lore of the bush and as simple, guileless savages fit only for carrying burdens. But the clients they serve are not quite like the sportsmen of Hemingway's time, since they are deads, and secretly the porters are terrified of the strange beings whom they serve. Sybille has seen them muttering prayers and fondling amulets whenever they accidentally touch one of the deads, and has occasionally detected an unguarded glance conveying unalloyed fear, possibly revulsion. Gracchus is no friend of theirs, however jolly he may get with them: they appear to regard him as some sort of monstrous sorcerer and the clients as fiends made manifest.

Sweating, saying little, the hunters move in single file, first the porters with the guns and supplies, then Gracchus, Zacharias, Sybille, Nerita constantly clicking her camera, and Mortimer. Patches of white cloud drift slowly across the immense arch of the sky. The grass is lush and thick, for the short rains were unusually heavy in December. Small animals scurry through it, visible only in quick flashes, squirrels and jackals and guinea-fowl. Now and then larger creatures can be seen: three haughty ostriches, a pair of snuffling hyenas, a band of Thomson gazelles flowing like a tawny river across the plain. Yesterday Sybille spied two wart hogs, some giraffes, and a serval, an elegant big-eared wildcat that slithered along like a miniature cheetah. None of these beasts may be hunted, but only those special ones that the operators of the preserve have introduced for the special needs of their clients; anything considered native African wildlife, which is to say anything that was living here before the deads leased this tract from the Masai, is protected by government

47

decree. The Masai themselves are allowed to do some lion-hunting, since this is their reservation, but there are so few Masai left that they can do little harm. Yesterday, after the wart hogs and before the giraffes, Sybille saw her first Masai, five lean, handsome, long-bodied men, naked under skimpy red robes, drifting silently through the bush, pausing frequently to stand thoughtfully on one leg, propped against their spears. At close range they were less handsome—toothless, fly-specked, herniated. They offered to sell their spears and their beaded collars for a few shillings, but the safarigoers had already stocked up on Masai artifacts in Nairobi's curio shops, at astonishingly higher prices.

All through the morning they stalk the quagga, Gracchus pointing out hoofprints here, fresh dung there. It is Zacharias who has asked to shoot a quagga. "How can you tell we're not following a zebra?" he asks peevishly.

Gracchus winks. "Trust me. We'll find zebras up ahead too. But you'll get your quagga. I guarantee it."

Ngiri, the head porter, turns and grins. "*Piga quagga m'uzuri bwana*," he says to Zacharias, and winks also, and then—Sybille sees it plainly—his jovial confident smile fades as though he has had the courage to sustain it only for an instant, and a veil of dread covers his dark glossy face.

"What did he say?" Zacharias asks.

"That you'll shoot a fine quagga," Gracchus replies.

Quaggas. The last wild one was killed about 1870, leaving only three in the world, all females, in European zoos. The Boers had hunted them to the edge of extinction in order to feed their tender meat to Hottentot slaves and to make from their striped hides sacks for Boer grain, leather *veldschoen* for Boer feet. The quagga of the London zoo died in 1872, that in Berlin in 1875, the Amsterdam quagga in 1883, and none was seen alive again until the artificial revival of the species through breedback selection and genetic manipulation in 2025, when this hunting preserve was opened to a limited and special clientele.

It is nearly noon, now, and not a shot has been fired all morning. The animals have begun heading for cover; they will not emerge until the shadows lengthen. Time to halt, pitch camp, break out the beer and sandwiches, tell tall tales of harrowing adventures with maddened buffaloes and edgy elephants. But not quite yet. The marchers come over a low hill and see, in the long sloping hollow beyond, a flock of ostriches and several hundred grazing zebras. As the humans appear, the ostriches begin slowly and warily to move off, but the zebras, altogether unafraid, continue to graze. Ngiri points and says, *"Piga quagga, bwana."*

"Just a bunch of zebras," Zacharias says.

Gracchus shakes his head. "No. Listen. You hear the sound?"

At first no one perceives anything unusual. But then, yes, Sybille hears it: a shrill barking neigh, very strange, a sound out of lost time, the cry of some beast she has never known. It is a song of the dead. Nerita hears it too, and Mortimer, and finally Zacharias. Gracchus nods toward the far side of the hollow. There, among the zebras, are half a dozen animals that might almost be zebras, but are not—unfinished zebras, striped only on their heads and foreparts; the rest of their bodies are yellowish brown, their legs are white, their manes are dark-brown with pale stripes. Their coats sparkle like mica in the sunshine. Now and again they lift their heads, emit that weird percussive whistling snort, and bend to the grass again. Quaggas. Strays out of the past, relicts, rekindled specters. Gracchus signals and the party fans out along the peak of the hill. Ngiri hands Zacharias his colossal gun. Zacharias kneels, sights.

"No hurry," Gracchus murmurs. "We have all afternoon."

"Do I seem to be hurrying?" Zacharias asks. The zebras now block the little group of quaggas from his view, almost as if by design. He must not shoot a zebra, of course, or there will be trouble with the rangers. Minutes go by. Then the screen of zebras abruptly parts and Zacharias squeezes his trigger. There is a vast explosion; zebras bolt in ten directions, so that the eye is bombarded with dizzying stroboscopic waves of black and white; when the convulsive confusion passes, one of the quaggas is lying on its side, alone in the field, having made the transition across the interface. Sybille regards it calmly. Death once dismayed her, death of any kind, but no longer.

"Paga m'uzuri!" the porters cry exultantly.

"Kufa," Gracchus says. "Dead. A neat shot. You have your trophy."

Ngiri is quick with the skinning-knife. That night, camping below Kilimanjaro's broad flank, they dine on roast quagga, deads and porters alike. The meat is juicy, robust, faintly tangy.

Late the following afternoon, as they pass through cooler stream-broken country thick with tall, scrubby gray-green vase-shaped trees, they come upon a monstrosity, a shaggy shambling thing twelve or fifteen feet high, standing upright on ponderous hind legs and balancing itself on an incredibly thick, heavy tail. It leans against a tree, pulling at its top branches with long forelimbs that are tipped with ferocious claws like a row of sickles; it munches voraciously on leaves and twigs. Briefly it notices them, and looks around, studying them with small stupid yellow eyes; then it returns to its meal.

"A rarity," Gracchus says. "I know hunters who have been all over this park without ever running into one. Have you ever seen anything so ugly?"

"What is it?" Sybille asks.

"Megatherium. Giant ground sloth. South American, really, but we weren't fussy about geography when we were stocking this place. We have only four of them, and it costs God knows how many thousands of dollars to shoot one. Nobody's signed up for a ground sloth yet. I doubt anyone will."

Sybille wonders where the beast might be vulnerable to a bullet: surely not in its dim peanut-sized brain. She wonders, too, what sort of sportsman would find pleasure in killing such a thing. For a while they watch as the sluggish monster tears the tree apart. Then they move on.

Gracchus shows them another prodigy at sundown: a pale dome, like some huge melon, nestling in a mound of dense grass beside a stream. "Ostrich egg?" Mortimer guesses.

"Close. Very close. It's a moa egg. World's biggest bird. From New Zealand, extinct since about the eighteenth century."

Nerita crouches and lightly taps the egg. "What an omelet we could make!"

"There's enough there to feed seventy-five of us," Gracchus says. "Two gallons of fluid, easy. But of course we mustn't meddle with it. Natural increase is very important in keeping this park stocked."

"And where's mama moa?" Sybille asks. "Should she have abandoned the egg?"

"Moas aren't very bright," Gracchus answers. "That's one good reason why they became extinct. She must have wandered off to find some dinner. And—"

"Good God," Zacharias blurts.

The moa has returned, emerging suddenly from a thicket. She stands like a feathered mountain above them, limned by the deep-blue of twilight: an ostrich, more or less, but a magnified ostrich, an ultimate ostrich, a bird a dozen feet high, with a heavy rounded body and a great thick hose of a neck and taloned legs sturdy as saplings. Surely this is Sinbad's rukh, that can fly off with elephants in its grasp! The bird peers at them, sadly contemplating the band of small beings clustered about her egg; she arches her neck as though readying for an attack, and Zacharias reaches for one of the rifles, but Gracchus checks his hand, for the moa is merely rearing back to protest. It utters a deep mournful mooing sound and does not move. "Just back slowly away," Gracchus tells them. "It won't attack. But keep away from the feet; one kick can kill you."

"I was going to apply for a license on a moa," Mortimer says.

"Killing them's a bore," Gracchus tells him. "They just stand there and let you shoot. You're better off with what you signed up for."

What Mortimer has signed up for is an aurochs, the vanished wild ox of the European forests, known to Caesar, known to Pliny, hunted by the hero Siegfried, altogether exterminated by the year 1627. The plains of East Africa are not a comfortable environment for the aurochs and the herd that has been conjured by the genetic necromancers keeps to itself in the wooded highlands, several days' journey from the haunts of quaggas and ground sloths. In this dark grove the hunters come upon troops of chattering baboons and solitary big-eared elephants and, in a place of broken sunlight and shadow, a splendid antelope, a bull bongo with a fine curving pair of horns. Gracchus leads them onward, deeper in. He seems tense: there is peril here. The porters slip through the forest like black wraiths, spreading out in arching crab-claw patterns, communicating with one another and with Gracchus by whistling. Everyone keeps weapons ready in here. Sybille half expects to see leopards draped on overhanging branches, cobras slithering through the undergrowth. But she feels no fear.

They approach a clearing.

"Aurochs," Gracchus says.

A dozen of them are cropping the shrubbery: big short-haired long-horned cattle, muscular and alert. Picking up the scent of the intruders, they lift their heavy heads, sniff, glare. Gracchus and Ngiri confer with eyebrows. Nodding, Gracchus mutters to Mortimer, "Too many of them. Wait for them to thin off." Mortimer smiles. He looks a little nervous. The aurochs has a reputation for attacking without warning. Four, five, six of the beasts slip away, and the others withdraw to the edge of the clearing, as if to plan strategy; but one big bull, sour-eyed and grim, stands his ground, glowering. Gracchus rolls on the balls of his feet. His burly body seems, to Sybille, a study in mobility, in preparedness.

"Now," he says.

In the same moment the bull aurochs charges, moving with extraordinary swiftness, head lowered, horns extended like spears. Mortimer fires. The bullet strikes with a loud whonking sound, crashing into the shoulder of the aurochs, a perfect shot, but the animal does not fall, and Mortimer shoots again, less gracefully ripping into the belly, and then Gracchus and Ngiri are firing also, not at Mortimer's aurochs but over the heads of the others, to drive them away, and the risky tactic works, for the other animals go stampeding off into the woods. The one Mortimer has shot continues toward him, staggering now, losing momentum, and falls practically at his feet, rolling over, knifing the forest floor with its hooves.

"*Kufa*," Ngiri says. "*Piga nyati m'uzuri, bwana.*"

Mortimer grins. "*Piga*," he says.

Gracchus salutes him. "More exciting than moa," he says.

"And these are mine," says Nerita three hours later, indicating a tree at the outer rim of the forest. Several hundred large pigeons nest in its boughs, so many of them that the tree seems to be sprouting birds rather than leaves. The females are plain—light-brown above, gray below—but the males are flamboyant, with rich, glossy blue plumage on their wings and backs, breasts of a wine-red chestnut color, iridescent spots of bronze and green on their necks, and weird, vivid eyes of a bright, fiery orange. Gracchus says, "Right. You've found your passenger pigeons."

"Where's the thrill in shooting pigeons out of a tree?" Mortimer asks.

Nerita gives him a withering look. "Where's the thrill in gunning down a charging bull?" She signals to Ngiri, who fires a shot into the air. The startled pigeons burst from their perches and fly in low circles. In the old days, a century and a half ago in the forests of North America, no one troubled to shoot passenger pigeons on the wing: the pigeons were food, not sport, and it was simpler to blast them as they sat, for that way a single hunter might kill thousands of birds in one day. Thus it took only fifty years to reduce the passenger pigeon population from uncountable sky-blackening billions to zero. Nerita is more sporting. This is a test of her skill, after all. She aims her shotgun, shoots, pumps, shoots, pumps. Stunned birds drop to the ground. She and her gun are a single entity, sharing one purpose. In moments it is all over. The porters retrieve the fallen birds and snap their necks. Nerita has the dozen pigeons her license allows: a pair to mount, the rest for tonight's dinner. The survivors have returned to their tree and stare placidly, unreproachfully, at the hunters.

"They breed so damned fast," Gracchus mutters. "If we aren't careful, they'll be getting out of the preserve and taking over all of Africa."

Sybille laughs. "Don't worry. We'll cope. We wiped them out once and we can do it again, if we have to."

Sybille's prey is a dodo. In Dar, when they were applying for their licenses, the others mocked her choice: a fat flightless bird, unable to run or fight, so feeble of wit that it fears nothing. She ignored them. She wants a dodo because to her it is the essence of extinction, the prototype of all that is dead and vanished. That there is no sport in shooting foolish dodos means little to Sybille. Hunting itself is meaningless for her.

Through this vast park she wanders as in a dream. She sees ground sloths, great auks, quaggas, moas, heath hens, Javan rhinos, giant armadillos, and many other rarities. The place is an abode of ghosts. The ingenuities of the genetic craftsmen are limitless; someday, perhaps, the preserve will offer trilobites, tyrannosaurs, mastodons, saber-toothed cats, baluchitheria, even—why not?— packs of Australopithecines, tribes of Neanderthals. For the amusement of the deads, whose games tend to be somber. Sybille wonders whether it can really be considered killing, this slaughter of laboratory-spawned novelties. Are these animals real or artificial? Living things, or cleverly animated constructs? Real, she decides. Living. They eat, they metabolize, they reproduce. They must seem real to themselves, and so they are real, realer, maybe, than dead human beings who walk again in their own cast-off bodies.

"Shotgun," Sybille says to the closest porter.

There is the bird, ugly, ridiculous, waddling laboriously through the tall grass. Sybille accepts a weapon and sights along its barrel. "Wait," Nerita says. "I'd like to get a picture of this." She moves slantwise around the group, taking exaggerated care not to frighten the dodo, but the dodo does not seem to be aware of any of them. Like an emissary from the realm of darkness, carrying good news of death to those creatures not yet extinct, it plods diligently across their path. "Fine," Nerita says. "Anthony, point at the dodo, will you, as if you've just noticed it? Kent, I'd like you to look down at your gun, study its bolt or something. Fine. And Sybille, just hold that pose—aiming—yes—"

Nerita takes the picture.

Calmly Sybille pulls the trigger.

"*Kazi imekwisha,*" Gracchus says. "The work is finished."

Six

Although to be driven back upon oneself is an uneasy affair at best, rather like trying to cross a border with borrowed credentials, it seems to be now the one condition necessary to the beginnings of real self-respect. Most of our platitudes notwithstanding, self-deception remains the most difficult deception. The tricks that work on others count for nothing in that very well-lit back alley where one keeps assignations with oneself: no winning smiles will do here, no prettily drawn lists of good intentions.

Joan Didion: *On Self-Respect*

"You better believe what Jeej is trying to tell you," Dolorosa said. "Ten minutes inside the Cold Town, they'll have your number. Five minutes."

Jijibhoi's man was small, rumpled-looking, forty or fifty years old, with untidy long dark hair and wide-set smoldering eyes. His skin was sallow and his face was gaunt. Such other deads as Klein had seen at close range had about them an air of unearthly serenity, but not this one: Dolorosa was tense, fidgety, a knuckle-cracker, a lip-gnawer. Yet somehow there could be no doubt he was a dead, as much a dead as Zacharias, as Gracchus, as Mortimer.

"They'll have my what?" Klein asked.

"Your number. Your number. They'll know you aren't a dead, because it can't be faked. Jesus, don't you even speak English? Jorge, that's a foreign name. I should have known. Where are you from?"

"Argentina, as a matter of fact, but I was brought to California when I was a small boy. In 1995. Look, if they catch me, they catch

55

me. I just want to get in there and spend half an hour talking with my wife."

"Mister, you don't have any wife any more."

"With Sybille," Klein said, exasperated. "To talk with Sybille, my—my former wife."

"All right. I'll get you inside."

"What will it cost?"

"Never mind that," Dolorosa said. "I owe Jeej here a few favors. More than a few. So I'll get you the drug—"

"Drug?"

"The drug the Treasury agents use when they infiltrate the Cold Towns. It narrows the pupils, contracts the capillaries, gives you that good old zombie look. The agents always get caught and thrown out, and so will you, but at least you'll go in there feeling that you've got a convincing disguise. Little oily capsule, one every morning before breakfast."

Klein looked at Jijibhoi. "Why do Treasury agents infiltrate the Cold Towns?"

"For the same reasons they infiltrate anywhere else," Jijibhoi said. "To spy. They are trying to compile dossiers on the financial dealings of the deads, you see, and until proper life-defining legislation is approved by Congress there is no precise way of compelling a person who is deemed legally dead to divulge—"

Dolorosa said, "Next, the background. I can get you a card of residence from Albany Cold Town in New York. You died last December, okay, and they rekindled you back east because—let's see—"

"I could have been attending the annual meeting of the American Historical Association in New York," Klein suggested. "That's what I do, you understand, professor of contemporary history at UCLA. Because of the Christmas holiday my body couldn't be shipped back to California, no room on any flight, and so they took me to Albany. How does that sound?"

Dolorosa smiled. "You really enjoy making up lies, Professor, don't you? I can dig that quality in you. Okay, Albany Cold Town, and this is your first trip out of there, your drying-off trip—that's what it's called, drying-off—you come out of the Cold Town like a new butterfly just out of its cocoon, all soft and damp, and you're on your own in a strange place. Now, there's a lot of stuff you'll need to know about how to behave, little mannerisms, social graces, that kind of crap, and I'll work on that with you tomorrow and Wednesday, and Friday, three sessions; that ought to be enough. Meanwhile let me give you the basics. There are only three things you really have to remember while you're inside:

"(1) Never ask a direct question.

"(2) Never lean on anybody's arm. You know what I mean?

"(3) Keep in mind that to a dead the whole universe is plastic, nothing's real, nothing matters a hell of a lot, it's all only a joke. Only a joke, friend, only a joke."

Early in April he flew to Salt Lake City, rented a car, and drove out past Moab into the high plateau rimmed by red-rock mountains where the deads had built Zion Cold Town. This was Klein's second visit to the necropolis. The other had been in the late summer of '31, a hot, parched season when the sun filled half the sky and even the gnarled junipers looked dazed from thirst; but now it was a frosty afternoon, with faint pale light streaming out of the wintry western hills and occasional gusts of light snow whirling through the iron-blue air. Jijibhoi's route instructions pulsed from the memo screen on his dashboard. Fourteen miles from town, yes, narrow paved lane turns off highway, yes, discreet little sign announcing PRIVATE ROAD, NO ADMITTANCE, yes, a second sign a thousand yards in, ZION COLD TOWN, MEMBERS ONLY, yes, and then just beyond that the barrier of green light across the road, the scanner system, the roadblocks sliding like scythes out of the underground installations, a voice on an invisible loudspeaker saying, "If you have a permit to enter Zion Cold Town, please place it under your left-hand windshield wiper."

That other time he had had no permit, and he had gone no farther than this, though at least he had managed a little colloquy with the unseen gatekeeper out of which he had squeezed the information that Sybille was indeed living in that particular Cold Town. This time he affixed Dolorosa's forged card of residence to his windshield, and waited tensely, and in thirty seconds the roadblocks slid from sight. He drove on, along a winding road that followed the natural contours of a dense forest of scrubby conifers, and came at last to a brick wall that curved away into the trees as though it encircled the entire town. Probably it did. Klein had an overpowering sense of the Cold Town as a hermetic city, ponderous and sealed as old Egypt. There was a metal gate in the brick wall; green electronic eyes surveyed him, signaled their approval, and the wall rolled open.

He drove slowly toward the center of town, passing through a zone of what he supposed were utility buildings—storage depots, a power substation, the municipal waterworks, whatever, a bunch of grim windowless one-story cinderblock affairs—and then into the residential district, which was not much lovelier. The streets were laid out on a rectangular grid; the buildings were squat, dreary, impersonal, homogeneous. There was practically no automobile traffic, and in a dozen blocks he saw no more than ten pedestrians, who did not even glance at him. So this was the environment in which the deads chose to spend their second lives. But why such deliberate bleakness? "You will never understand us," Dolorosa had warned. Dolorosa was right. Jijibhoi had told him that Cold Towns were something less than charming, but Klein had not been prepared for this. There was a glacial quality about the place, as though it were wholly entombed in a block of clear ice: silence, sterility, a mortuary calm. Cold Town, yes, aptly named. Architecturally, the town looked like the worst of all possible cheap-and-sleazy tract developments, but the psychic texture it projected was even more depressing, more like that of one of those ghastly retirement communities, one of the innumerable Leisure Worlds or Sun Manors, those childless joyless retreats where colonies of that other kind of living dead collected to await the last trumpet. Klein shivered.

At last, another few minutes deeper into the town, a sign of activity, if not exactly of life: a shopping center, flat-topped brown stucco buildings around a U-shaped courtyard, a steady flow of shoppers moving about. All right. His first test was about to commence. He parked his car near the mouth of the U and strolled uneasily inward. He felt as if his forehead were a beacon, flashing glowing betrayals at rhythmic intervals:

FRAUD   INTRUDER   INTERLOPER   SPY

Go ahead, he thought, seize me, seize the impostor, get it over with, throw me out, string me up, crucify me. But no one seemed to pick up the signals. He was altogether ignored. Out of courtesy? Or just contempt? He stole what he hoped were covert glances at the shoppers, half expecting to run across Sybille right away. They all looked like sleepwalkers, moving in glazed silence about their errands. No smiles, no chatter: the icy aloofness of these self-contained people heightened the familiar suburban atmosphere of the shopping center into surrealist intensity, Norman Rockwell with an overlay of Dali or De Chirico. The shopping center looked like all other shopping centers: clothing stores, a bank, a record shop, snack bars, a florist, a TV/stereo outlet, a theater, a five-and-dime. One difference, though, became apparent as Klein wandered from shop to shop: the whole place was automated. There were no clerks anywhere, only the ubiquitous data screens, and no doubt a battery of hidden scanners to discourage shoplifters. (Or did the impulse toward petty theft perish with the body's first death?) The customers selected all the merchandise themselves, checked it out via data screens, touched their thumbs to chargeplates to debit their accounts. Of course. No one was going to waste his precious rekindled existence standing behind a counter to sell tennis shoes or cotton candy. Nor were the dwellers in the Cold Towns likely to dilute their isolation by hiring a labor force of imported warms. Somebody here had to do a little work, obviously—how did the merchandise get into the stores?—but, in general, Klein realized, what could not be done here by machines would not be done at all.

For ten minutes he prowled the center. Just when he was beginning to think he must be entirely invisible to these people, a short, broad-shouldered man, bald but with oddly youthful features, paused in front of him and said, "I am Pablo. I welcome you to Zion Cold Town." This unexpected puncturing of the silence so startled Klein that he had to fight to retain appropriate deadlike imperturbability. Pablo smiled warmly and touched both his hands to Klein's in friendly greeting, but his eyes were frigid, hostile, remote, a terrifying contradiction. "I've been sent to bring you to the lodging-place. Come: your car."

Other than to give directions, Pablo spoke only three times during the five-minute drive. "Here is the rekindling house," he said. A five-story building, as inviting as a hospital, with walls of dark bronze and windows black as onyx. "This is Guidefather's house," Pablo said a moment later. A modest brick building, like a rectory, at the edge of a small park. And, finally: "This is where you will stay. Enjoy your visit." Abruptly he got out of the car and walked rapidly away.

This was the house of strangers, the hotel for visiting deads, a long low cinderblock structure, functional and unglamorous, one of the least seductive buildings in this city of stark disagreeable buildings. However else it might be with the deads, they clearly had no craving for fancy architecture. A voice out of a data screen in the spartan lobby assigned him to a room: a white-walled box, square, high of ceiling. He had his own toilet, his own data screen, a narrow bed, a chest of drawers, a modest closet, a small window that gave him a view of a neighboring building just as drab as this. Nothing had been said about rental; perhaps he was a guest of the city. Nothing had been said about anything. It seemed that he had been accepted. So much for Jijibhoi's gloomy assurance that he would instantly be found out, so much for Dolorosa's insistence that they would have his number in ten minutes or less. He had been in Zion Cold Town for half an hour. Did they have his number?

"Eating isn't important among us," Dolorosa had said.
"But you do eat?"
"Of course we eat. It just isn't *important*."
It was important to Klein, though. Not haute cuisine, necessarily, but some sort of food, preferably three times a day. He was getting hungry now. Ring for room service? There were no servants in this city. He turned to the data screen. Dolorosa's first rule: *Never ask a direct question.* Surely that didn't apply to the data screen, only to his fellow deads. He didn't have to observe the niceties of etiquette when talking to a computer. Still, the voice behind the screen might not be that of a computer after all, so he tried to employ the

oblique, elliptical conversational style that Dolorosa said the deads favored among themselves:

"Dinner?"

"Commissary."

"Where?"

"Central Four," said the screen.

Central Four? All right. He would find the way. He changed into fresh clothing and went down the long vinyl-floored hallway to the lobby. Night had come; street lamps were glowing; under cloak of darkness the city's ugliness was no longer so obtrusive, and there was even a kind of controlled beauty about the brutal regularity of its streets.

The streets were unmarked, though, and deserted. Klein walked at random for ten minutes, hoping to meet someone heading for the Central Four commissary. But when he did come upon someone, a tall and regal woman well advanced in years, he found himself incapable of approaching her. (*Never ask a direct question. Never lean on anybody's arm.*) He walked alongside her, in silence and at a distance, until she turned suddenly to enter a house. For ten minutes more he wandered alone again. This is ridiculous, he thought: dead or warm, I'm a stranger in town, I should be entitled to a little assistance. Maybe Dolorosa was just trying to complicate things. On the next corner, when Klein caught sight of a man hunched away from the wind, lighting a cigarette, he went boldly over to him. "Excuse me, but—"

The other looked up. "Klein?" he said. "Yes. Of course. Well, so you've made the crossing too!"

He was one of Sybille's Zanzibar companions, Klein realized. The quick-eyed, sharp-edged one—Mortimer. A member of her pseudo-familial grouping, whatever that might be. Klein stared sullenly at him. This had to be the moment when his imposture would be exposed, for only some six weeks had passed since he had argued with Mortimer in the gardens of Sybille's Zanzibar hotel, not nearly enough time for someone to have died and been rekindled and gone through his drying-off. But a moment passed and Mortimer said nothing. At length Klein said, "I just got here. Pablo showed me to the house of strangers and now I'm looking for the commissary."

"Central Four? I'm going there myself. How lucky for you." No sign of suspicion in Mortimer's face. Perhaps an elusive smile revealed his awareness that Klein could not be what he claimed to be. *Keep in mind that to a dead the whole universe is plastic, it's all only a joke.* "I'm waiting for Nerita," Mortimer said. "We can all eat together."

Klein said heavily, "I was rekindled in Albany Cold Town. I've just emerged."

"How nice," Mortimer said.

Nerita Tracy stepped out of a building just beyond the corner—a slim, athletic-looking woman, about forty, with short reddish-brown hair. As she swept toward them, Mortimer said, "Here's Klein, who we met in Zanzibar. Just rekindled, out of Albany."

"Sybille will be amused."

"Is she in town?" Klein blurted.

Mortimer and Nerita exchanged sly glances. Klein felt abashed. *Never ask a direct question.* Damn Dolorosa!

Nerita said, "You'll see her before long. Shall we go to dinner?"

The commissary was less austere than Klein had expected: actually quite an inviting restaurant, elaborately constructed on five or six levels divided by lustrous dark hangings into small, secluded dining areas. It had the warm, rich look of a tropical resort.

But the food, which came automat-style out of revolving dispensers, was prefabricated and cheerless—another jarring contradiction. *Only a joke, friend, only a joke.* In any case he was less hungry than he had imagined at the hotel. He sat with Mortimer and Nerita, picking at his meal, while their conversation flowed past him at several times the speed of thought. They spoke in fragments and ellipses, in periphrastics and aposiopeses, in a style abundant in chiasmus, metonymy, meiosis, oxymoron, and zeugma; their dazzling rhetorical techniques left him baffled and uncomfortable, which beyond much doubt was their intention. Now and again they would dart from a thicket of indirection to skewer him with a quick corroborative stab: Isn't that so, they would say, and he would smile and nod, nod and smile, saying, Yes, yes, absolutely. Did they know he was a fake, and were they merely playing with him, or had they, somehow, impossibly, accepted him as one of them? So subtle was their style that he could not tell.

A very new member of the society of the rekindled, he told himself, would be nearly as much at sea here as a warm in deadface.

Then Nerita said—no verbal games, this time—"You still miss her terribly, don't you?"

"I do. Some things evidently never perish."

"Everything perishes," Mortimer said. "The dodo, the aurochs, the Holy Roman Empire, the T'ang Dynasty, the walls of Byzantium, the language of Mohenjo-daro."

"But not the Great Pyramid, the Yangtze, the coelacanth, or the skullcap of Pithecanthropus," Klein countered. "Some things persist and endure. And some can be regenerated. Lost languages have been deciphered. I believe the dodo and the aurochs are hunted in a certain African park in this very era."

"Replicas," Mortimer said.

"Convincing replicas. Simulations as good as the original."

"Is that what you want?" Nerita asked.

"I want what's possible to have."

"A convincing replica of lost love?"

"I might be willing to settle for five minutes of conversation with her."

"You'll have it. Not tonight. See? There she is. But don't bother her now." Nerita nodded across the gulf in the center of the restaurant; on the far side, three levels up from where they sat, Sybille and Kent Zacharias had appeared. They stood for a brief while at the edge of their dining alcove, staring blandly and emotionlessly into the restaurant's central well. Klein felt a muscle jerking uncontrollably in his cheek, a damning revelation of undeadlike uncoolness, and pressed his hand over it, so that it twanged and throbbed against his palm. She was like a goddess up there, manifesting herself in her sanctum to her worshipers, a pale shimmering figure, more beautiful even than she had become to him through the anguished enhancements of memory, and it seemed impossible to him that that being had ever been his wife, that he had known her when her eyes were puffy and reddened from a night of study, that he had looked down at her face as they made love and had seen her lips pull back in that spasm of ecstasy that is so close to a grimace of pain, that he had known her crotchety and unkind in her illness, short-tempered

63

and impatient in health, a person of flaws and weaknesses, of odors and blemishes, in short a human being, this goddess, this unreal rekindled creature, this object of his quest, this Sybille. Serenely she turned, serenely she vanished into her cloaked alcove. "She knows you're here," Nerita told him. "You'll see her. Perhaps tomorrow." Then Mortimer said something maddeningly oblique, and Nerita replied with the same off-center mystification, and Klein once more was plunged into the river of their easy dancing wordplay, down into it, down and down and down, and as he struggled to keep from drowning, as he fought to comprehend their interchanges, he never once looked toward the place where Sybille sat, not even once, and congratulated himself on having accomplished that much at least in his masquerade.

That night, lying alone in his room at the house of strangers, he wonders what he will say to Sybille when they finally meet, and what she will say to him. Will he dare bluntly to ask her to describe to him the quality of her new existence? That is all that he wants from her, really, that knowledge, that opening of an aperture into her transfigured self; that is as much as he hopes to get from her, knowing as he does that there is scarcely a chance of regaining her, but will he dare to ask, will he dare even that? Of course his asking such things will reveal to her that he is still a warm, too dense and gross of perception to comprehend the life of a dead; but he is certain she will sense that anyway, instantly. What will he say, what will he say? He plays out an imagined script of their conversation in the theater of his mind:

—Tell me what it's like, Sybille, to be the way you are now.

—Like swimming under a sheet of glass.

—I don't follow.

—Everything is quiet where I am, Jorge. There's a peace that passeth all understanding. I used to feel sometimes that I was caught up in a great storm, that I was being buffeted by every breeze, that my life was being consumed by agitations and frenzies, but now, now, I'm at the eye of the storm, at the place where everything is always calm. I observe rather than let myself be acted upon.

—But isn't there a loss of feeling that way? Don't you feel that you're wrapped in an insulating layer? Like swimming, under glass, you say—that conveys being insulate, being cut off, being almost numb.

—I suppose you might think so. The way it is, is that one no longer is affected by the unnecessary.

—It sounds to me like a limited existence.

—Less limited than the grave, Jorge.

—I never understood why you wanted rekindling. You were such a world-devourer, Sybille, you lived with such intensity, such passion. To settle for the kind of existence you have now, to be only half-alive—

—Don't be a fool, Jorge. To be half-alive is better than to be rotting in the ground. I was so young. There was so much else still to see and do.

—But to see it and do it half-alive?

—Those were your words, not mine. I'm not alive at all. I'm neither less nor more than the person you knew. I'm another kind of being altogether. Neither less nor more, only different.

—Are all your perceptions different?

—Very much so. My perspective is broader. Little things stand revealed as little things.

—Give me an example, Sybille.

—I'd rather not. How could I make anything clear to you? Die and be with us, and you'll understand.

—You know I'm not dead?

—Oh, Jorge, how funny you are!

—How nice that I can still amuse you.

—You look so hurt, so tragic. I could almost feel sorry for you. Come: ask me anything.

—Could you leave your companions and live in the world again?

—I've never considered that.

—Could you?

—I suppose I could. But why should I? This is my world now.

—This ghetto.

—Is that how it seems to you?

65

—You lock yourselves into a closed society of your peers, a tight subculture. Your own jargon, your own wall of etiquette and idiosyncrasy. Designed, I think, mainly to keep the outsiders off balance, to keep them feeling like outsiders. It's a defensive thing. The hippies, the blacks, the gays, the deads—same mechanism, same process.

—The Jews, too. Don't forget the Jews.

—All right, Sybille, the Jews. With their little tribal jokes, their special holidays, their own mysterious language, yes, a good case in point.

—So I've joined a new tribe. What's wrong with that?

—Did you need to be part of a tribe?

—What did I have before? The tribe of Californians? The tribe of academics?

—The tribe of Jorge and Sybille Klein.

—Too narrow. Anyway, I've been expelled from that tribe. I needed to join another one.

—Expelled?

—By death. After that there's no going back.

—You could go back. Any time.

—Oh, no, no, no, Jorge, I can't; I can't, I'm not Sybille Klein any more, I never will be again. How can I explain it to you? There's no way. Death brings on changes. Die and see, Jorge. Die and see.

Nerita said, "She's waiting for you in the lounge."

It was a big, coldly furnished room at the far end of the other wing of the house of strangers. Sybille stood by a window through which pale, chilly morning light was streaming. Mortimer was with her, and also Kent Zacharias. The two men favored Klein with mysterious oblique smiles—courteous or derisive, he could not tell which. "Do you like our town?" Zacharias asked. "Have you been seeing the sights?" Klein chose not to reply. He acknowledged the question with a faint nod and turned to Sybille. Strangely, he felt altogether calm at this moment of attaining a years-old desire: he felt nothing at all in her presence, no panic, no yearning, no dismay, no nostalgia, nothing, nothing. As though he were truly a dead. He knew it was the tranquility of utter terror.

"We'll leave you two alone," Zacharias said. "You must have so much to tell each other." He went out, with Nerita and Mortimer. Klein's eyes met Sybille's and lingered there. She was looking at him coolly, in a kind of impersonal appraisal. That damnable smile of hers, Klein thought: dying turns them all into Mona Lisas.

She said, "Do you plan to stay here long?"

"Probably not. A few days, maybe a week." He moistened his lips. "How have you been, Sybille? How has it been going?"

"It's all been about as I expected."

What do you mean by that? Can you give me some details? Are you at all disappointed? Have there been any surprises? What has it been like for you, Sybille? Oh, Jesus—

—Never ask a direct question—

He said, "I wish you had let me visit with you in Zanzibar."

"That wasn't possible. Let's not talk about it now." She dismissed the episode with a casual wave. After a moment she said, "Would you like to hear a fascinating story I've uncovered about the early days of Omani influence in Zanzibar?"

The impersonality of the question startled him. How could she display such absolute lack of curiosity about his presence in Zion Cold Town, his claim to be a dead, his reasons for wanting to see her? How could she plunge so quickly, so coldly, into a discussion of archaic political events in Zanzibar?

"I suppose so," he said weakly.

"It's a sort of Arabian Nights story, really. It's the story of how Ahmad the Sly overthrew Abdullah ibn Muhammad Alawi."

The names were strange to him. He had indeed taken some small part in her historical researches, but it was years since he had worked with her, and everything had drifted about in his mind, leaving a jumbled residue of Ahmads and Hasans and Abdullahs. "I'm sorry," he said. "I don't recall who they were."

Unperturbed, Sybille said, "Certainly you remember that in the eighteenth and early nineteenth centuries the chief power in the Indian Ocean was the Arab state of Oman, ruled from Muscat on the Persian Gulf. Under the Busaidi dynasty, founded in 1744 by Ahmad ibn Said al-Busaidi, the Omani extended their power to East Africa. The logical capital for their African empire was the port of Mombasa, but they were unable to evict a rival dynasty reigning there, so the Busaidi looked toward nearby Zanzibar—a cosmopolitan island of mixed Arab, Indian, and African population. Zanzibar's strategic placement on the coast and its spacious and well-protected harbor made it an ideal base for the East African slave trade that the Busaidi of Oman intended to dominate."

"It comes back to me now, I think."

"Very well. The founder of the Omani Sultanate of Zanzibar was Ahmad ibn Majid the Sly, who came to the throne of Oman in 1811—do you remember?—upon the death of his uncle Abd-er-Rahman al-Busaidi."

"The names sound familiar," Klein said doubtfully.

"Seven years later," Sybille continued, "seeking to conquer Zanzibar without the use of force, Ahmad the Sly shaved his beard and mustache and visited the island disguised as a soothsayer, wearing yellow robes and a costly emerald in his turban. At that time most of Zanzibar was governed by a native ruler of mixed Arab and African blood, Abdullah ibn Muhammad Alawi, whose hereditary title was Mwenyi Mkuu. The Mwenyi Mkuu's subjects were mainly Africans, members of a tribe called the Hadimu. Sultan Ahmad, arriving in Zanzibar Town, gave a demonstration of his soothsaying skills on the waterfront and attracted so much attention that he speedily gained an audience at the court of the Mwenyi Mkuu. Ahmad predicted a glowing future for Abdullah, declaring that a powerful prince famed throughout the world would come to Zanzibar, make the Mwenyi Mkuu his high lieutenant, and confirm him and his descendants as lords of Zanzibar forever.

"'How do you know these things?' asked the Mwenyi Mkuu.

"'There is a potion I drink,' Sultan Ahmad replied, 'that enables me to see what is to come. Do you wish to taste of it?'

"'Most surely I do,' Abdullah said, and Ahmad thereupon gave him a drug that sent him into rapturous transports and showed him visions of paradise. Looking down from his place near the footstool of Allah, the Mwenyi Mkuu saw a rich and happy Zanzibar governed by his children's children's children. For hours he wandered in fantasies of almighty power.

"Ahmad then departed, and let his beard and mustache grow again, and returned to Zanzibar ten weeks later in his full regalia as Sultan of Oman, at the head of an imposing and powerful armada. He went at once to the court of the Mwenyi Mkuu and proposed, just as the soothsayer had prophesied, that Oman and Zanzibar enter into a treaty of alliance under which Oman would assume responsibility for much of Zanzibar's external relations—including the slave trade—while guaranteeing the authority of the Mwenyi Mkuu over domestic affairs. In return for his partial abdication of authority, the Mwenyi Mkuu would receive financial compensation from Oman. Remembering the vision the soothsayer had revealed to him, Abdullah at once signed the treaty, thereby legitimizing what was, in effect, the Omani conquest of Zanzibar. A great feast was held to celebrate the treaty, and, as a mark of honor, the Mwenyi Mkuu offered Sultan Ahmad a rare drug used locally, known as *borqash*, or 'the flower of truth.' Ahmad only pretended to put the pipe to his lips, for he loathed all mind-altering drugs, but Abdullah, as the flower of truth possessed him, looked at Ahmad and recognized the outlines of the soothsayer's face behind the Sultan's new beard. Realizing that he had been deceived, the Mwenyi Mkuu thrust his dagger, the tip of which was poisoned, deep into the Sultan's side and fled the banquet hall, taking up residence on the neighboring island of Pemba. Ahmad ibn Majid survived, but the poison consumed his vital organs and the remaining ten years of his life were spent in constant agony. As for the Mwenyi Mkuu, the Sultan's men hunted him down and put him to death along with ninety members of his family, and native rule in Zanzibar was therewith extinguished."

Sybille paused. "Is that not a gaudy and wonderful story?" she asked at last.

"Fascinating," Klein said. "Where did you find it?"

"Unpublished memoirs of Claude Richburn of the East India Company. Buried deep in the London archives. Strange that no historian ever came upon it before, isn't it? The standard texts simply say that Ahmad used his navy to bully Abdullah into signing the treaty, and then had the Mwenyi Mkuu assassinated at the first convenient moment."

69

"Very strange," Klein agreed. But he had not come here to listen to romantic tales of visionary potions and royal treacheries. He groped for some way to bring the conversation to a more personal level. Fragments of his imaginary dialogue with Sybille floated through his mind. *Everything is quiet where I am, Jorge. There's a peace that passeth all understanding. Like swimming under a sheet of glass. The way it is, is that one no longer is affected by the unnecessary. Little things stand revealed as little things. Die and be with us, and you'll understand.* Yes. Perhaps. But did she really believe any of that? He had put all the words in her mouth; everything he had imagined her to say was his own construct, worthless as a key to the true Sybille. Where would he find the key, though?

She gave him no chance. "I will be going back to Zanzibar soon," she said. "There's much I want to learn about this incident from the people in the back country—old legends about the last days of the Mwenyi Mkuu, perhaps variants on the basic story—"

"May I accompany you?"

"Don't you have your own research to resume, Jorge?" she asked, and did not wait for an answer. She walked briskly toward the door of the lounge and went out, and he was alone.

Seven

I mean what they and their hired psychiatrists call "delusional systems." Needless to say, "delusions" are always officially defined. We don't have to worry about questions of real or unreal. They only talk out of expediency. It's the *system* that matters. How the data arrange themselves inside it. Some are consistent, others fall apart.

Thomas Pynchon: *Gravity's Rainbow*

Once more the deads, this time only three of them, coming over on the morning flight from Dar. Three was better than five, Daud Mahmoud Barwani supposed, but three was still more than a sufficiency. Not that those others, two months back, had caused any trouble, staying just the one day and flitting off to the mainland again, but it made him uncomfortable to think of such creatures on the same small island as himself. With all the world to choose, why did they keep coming to Zanzibar?

"The plane is here," said the flight controller.

Thirteen passengers. The health officer let the local people through the gate first—two newspapermen and four legislators coming back from the Pan-African Conference in Capetown—and then processed a party of four Japanese tourists, unsmiling owlish men festooned with cameras. And then the deads: and Barwani was surprised to discover that they were the same ones as before, the red-haired man, the brown-haired man without the beard, the black-haired woman. Did deads have so much money that they could fly from America to Zanzibar every few months? Barwani had heard a tale to the effect that each new dead, when he rose from his coffin, was presented with

71

bars of gold equal to his own weight, and now he thought he believed it. No good will come of having such beings loose in the world, he told himself, and certainly none from letting them into Zanzibar. Yet he had no choice. "Welcome once again to the isle of cloves," he said unctuously, and smiled a bureaucratic smile, and wondered, not for the first time, what would become of Daud Mahmoud Barwani once his days on earth had reached their end.

"—Ahmad the Sly versus Abdullah Something," Klein said. "That's all she would talk about. The history of Zanzibar." He was in Jijibhoi's study. The night was warm and a late-season rain was falling, blurring the million sparkling lights of the Los Angeles basin. "It would have been, you know, gauche to ask her any direct questions. Gauche. I haven't felt so gauche since I was fourteen. I was helpless among them, a foreigner, a child."

"Do you think they saw through your disguise?" Jijibhoi asked.

"I can't tell. They seemed to be toying with me, to be having sport with me, but that may just have been their general style with any newcomer. Nobody challenged me. Nobody hinted I might be an impostor. Nobody seemed to care very much about me or what I was doing there or how I had happened to become a dead. Sybille and I stood face to face, and I wanted to reach out to her, I wanted her to reach out to me, and there was no contact, none, none at all, it was as though we had just met at some academic cocktail party and the only thing on her mind was the new nugget of obscure history she had just unearthed, and so she told me all about how Sultan Ahmad outfoxed Abdullah and Abdullah stabbed the Sultan." Klein caught sight of a set of familiar books on Jijibhoi's crowded shelves—Oliver and Mathew, *History of East Africa,* books that had traveled everywhere with Sybille in the years of their marriage. He pulled forth Volume I, saying, "She claimed that the standard histories give a sketchy and inaccurate description of the incident and that she's only now discovered the true story. For all I know, she was just playing a game with me, telling me a piece of established history as though it were something nobody knew till last week. Let me see—Ahmad, Ahmad, Ahmad—"

He examined the index. Five Ahmads were listed, but there was no entry for a Sultan Ahmad ibn Majid the Sly. Indeed, an Ahmad ibn Majid was cited, but he was mentioned only in a footnote and appeared to be an Arab chronicler. Klein found three Abdullahs, none of them a man of Zanzibar. "Something's wrong," he murmured.

"It does not matter, dear Jorge," Jijibhoi said mildly.

"It does. Wait a minute." He prowled the listings. Under *Zanzibar, Rulers,* he found no Ahmads, no Abdullahs; he did discover a Majid ibn Said, but when he checked the reference he found that he had reigned somewhere in the second half of the nineteenth century. Desperately Klein flipped pages, skimming, turning back, searching. Eventually he looked up and said, "It's all wrong!"

"The Oxford *History of East Africa?*"

"The details of Sybille's story. Look, she said this Ahmad the Sly gained the throne of Oman in 1811, and seized Zanzibar seven years later. But the book says that a certain Seyyid Said al-Busaidi became Sultan of Oman in 1806, and ruled for *fifty years*. He was the one, not this nonexistent Ahmad the Sly, who grabbed Zanzibar, but he did it in 1828, and the ruler he compelled to sign a treaty with him, the Mwenyi Mkuu, was named Hasan ibn Ahmad Alawi, and—" Klein shook his head. "It's an altogether different cast of characters. No stabbings, no assassinations, the dates are entirely different, the whole thing—"

Jijibhoi smiled sadly. "The deads are often mischievous."

"But why would she invent a complete fantasy and palm it off as a sensational new discovery? Sybille was the most scrupulous scholar I ever knew! She would never—"

"That was the Sybille you knew, dear friend. I keep urging you to realize that this is another person, a new person, within her body."

"A person who would lie about history?"

"A person who would tease," Jijibhoi said.

"Yes," Klein muttered. "Who would tease." *Keep in mind that to a dead the whole universe is plastic, nothing's real, nothing matters a hell of a lot.* "Who would tease a stupid, boring, annoyingly persistent ex-husband who has shown up in her Cold Town, wearing a transparent disguise and pretending to be a dead. Who would invent not only an anecdote but even its principals, as a joke, a game, a *jeu d'esprit.* Oh, God. Oh, God, how cruel she is, how foolish I was! It was her way of telling me she knew I was a phony dead. Quid pro quo, fraud for fraud!"

73

"What will you do?"

"I don't know," Klein said.

What he did, against Jijibhoi's strong advice and his own better judgment, was to get more pills from Dolorosa and return to Zion Cold Town. There would be a fitful joy, like that of probing the socket of a missing tooth, in confronting Sybille with the evidence of her fictional Ahmad, her imaginary Abdullah. Let there be no more games between us, he would say. Tell me what I need to know, Sybille, and then let me go away; but tell me only truth. All the way to Utah he rehearsed his speech, polishing and embellishing. There was no need for it, though, since this time the gate of Zion Cold Town would not open for him. The scanners scanned his forged Albany card and the loudspeaker said, "Your credentials are invalid."

Which could have ended it. He might have returned to Los Angeles and picked up the pieces of his life. All this semester he had been on sabbatical leave, but the summer term was coming and there was work to do. He did return to Los Angeles, but only long enough to pack a somewhat larger suitcase, find his passport, and drive to the airport. On a sweet May evening a British Airways jet took him over the Pole to London, where, barely pausing for coffee and buns at an airport shop, he boarded another plane that carried him southeast toward Africa. More asleep than awake, he watched the dreamy landmarks drifting past: the Mediterranean, coming and going with surprising rapidity, and the tawny carpet of the Libyan Desert, and the mighty Nile, reduced to a brown thread's thickness when viewed from a height of ten miles. Suddenly Kilimanjaro, mist-wrapped, snow-bound, loomed like a giant double-headed blister to his right, far below, and he thought he could make out to his left the distant glare of the sun on the Indian Ocean. Then the big needle-nosed plane began its abrupt swooping descent, and he found himself, soon after, stepping out into the warm humid air and dazzling sunlight of Dar es Salaam.

Too soon, too soon. He felt unready to go on to Zanzibar. A day or two of rest, perhaps: he picked a Dar hotel at random, the Agip, liking the strange sound of its name, and hired a taxi. The hotel was sleek and clean, a streamlined affair in the glossy 2020s style, much cheaper than the Kilimanjaro, where he had stayed briefly on the other trip, and located in a pleasant leafy quarter of the city, near the ocean. He strolled about for a short while, discovered that he was altogether exhausted, returned to his room for a nap that stretched on for nearly five hours, and awakening groggy, showered and dressed for dinner. The hotel's dining room was full of beefy red-faced fair-haired men, jacketless and wearing open-throated white shirts, all of whom reminded him disturbingly of Kent Zacharias; but these were warms, Britishers from their accents, engineers, he suspected, from their conversation. They were building a dam and a power plant somewhere up the coast, it seemed, or perhaps a power plant without a dam; it was hard to follow what they said. They drank a good deal of gin and spoke in hearty booming shouts. There were also a good many Japanese businessmen, of course, looking trim and restrained in dark-blue suits and narrow ties, and at the table next to Klein's were five tanned curly-haired men talking in rapid Hebrew—Israelis, surely. The only Africans in sight were waiters and bartenders. Klein ordered Mombasa oysters, steak, and a carafe of red wine, and found the food unexpectedly good, but left most of it on his plate. It was late evening in Tanzania, but for him it was ten o'clock in the morning, and his body was confused. He tumbled into bed, meditated vaguely on the probable presence of Sybille just a few air-minutes away in Zanzibar, and dropped into a sound sleep from which he awakened, what seemed like many hours later, to discover that it was still well before dawn.

He dawdled away the morning sightseeing in the old native quarter, hot and dusty, with unpaved streets and rows of tin shacks, and at midday returned to his hotel for a shower and lunch. Much the same national distribution in the restaurant—British, Japanese, Israeli—though the faces seemed different. He was on his second beer when Anthony Gracchus came in. The white hunter, broad-shouldered, pale, densely bearded, clad in khaki shorts, khaki shirt, seemed almost to have stepped out of the picture-cube Jijibhoi had once shown him. Instinctively Klein shrank back, turning toward the window, but too late: Gracchus had seen him. All chatter came to a halt in the restaurant as the dead man strode to Klein's table, pulled out a chair unasked, and seated himself; then, as though a motion-picture projector had been halted and started again, the British engineers resumed their shouting, sounding somewhat strained now. "Small world," Gracchus said. "Crowded one, anyway. On your way to Zanzibar, are you, Klein?"

"In a day or so. Did you know I was here?"

"Of course not." Gracchus' harsh eyes twinkled slyly. "Sheer coincidence is what this is. She's there already."

"She is?"

"She and Zacharias and Mortimer. I hear you wiggled your way into Zion."

"Briefly," Klein said. "I saw Sybille. Briefly."

"Unsatisfactorily. So once again you've followed her here. Give it up, man. Give it up."

"I can't."

"*Can't!*" Gracchus scowled. "A neurotic's word, can't. What you mean is *won't*. A mature man can do anything he wants to that isn't a physical impossibility. Forget her. You're only annoying her, this way, interfering with her work, interfering with her—" Gracchus smiled. "With her life. She's been dead almost three years, hasn't she? Forget her. The world's full of other women. You're still young, you have money, you aren't ugly, you have professional standing—"

"Is this what you were sent here to tell me?"

"I wasn't sent here to tell you anything, friend. I'm only trying to save you from yourself. Don't go to Zanzibar. Go home and start your life again."

"When I saw her at Zion," Klein said, "she treated me with contempt. She amused herself at my expense. I want to ask her why she did that."

"Because you're a warm and she's a dead. To her you're a clown. To all of us you're a clown. It's nothing personal, Klein. There's simply a gulf in attitudes, a gulf too wide for you to cross. You went to Zion drugged up like a Treasury man, didn't you? Pale face, bulgy eyes? You didn't fool anyone. You certainly didn't fool *her*. The game she played with you was her way of telling you that. Don't you know that?"

"I know it, yes."

"What more do you want, then? More humiliation?"

Klein shook his head wearily and stared at the tablecloth. After a moment he looked up, and his eyes met those of Gracchus, and he was astounded to realize that he trusted the hunter, that for the first time in his dealings with the deads he felt he was being met with sincerity. He said in a low voice, "We were very close, Sybille and I, and then she died, and now I'm nothing to her. I haven't been able to come to terms with that. I need her, still. I want to share my life with her, even now."

"But you can't."

"I know that. And still I can't help doing what I've been doing."

"There's only one thing you *can* share with her," Gracchus said. "That's your death. She won't descend to your level: you have to climb to hers."

"Don't be absurd."

"Who's absurd, me or you? Listen to me, Klein. I think you're a fool, I think you're a weakling, but I don't dislike you, I don't hold you to blame for your own foolishness. And so I'll help you, if you'll allow me." He reached into his breast pocket and withdrew a tiny metal tube with a safety catch at one end. "Do you know what this is?" Gracchus asked. "It's a self-defense dart, the kind all the women in New York carry. A good many deads carry them, too, because we never know when the reaction will start, when the mobs will turn against us. Only we don't use anesthetic drugs in ours. Listen, we can walk into any tavern in the native quarter and have a decent brawl going in five minutes, and in the confusion I'll put one of these darts into you, and we'll have you in Dar General Hospital fifteen minutes after that, crammed into a deep-freeze unit, and for a few thousand dollars we can ship you unthawed to California, and this time Friday night you'll be undergoing rekindling in, say, San Diego Cold Town. And when you come out of it you and Sybille will be on the same side of the gulf, do you see? If you're destined to get back together with her, ever, that's the only way. That way you have a chance. This way you have none."

"It's unthinkable," Klein said.

"Unacceptable, maybe. But not unthinkable. Nothing's unthinkable once somebody's thought it. You think it some more. Will you promise me that? Think about it before you get aboard that plane for Zanzibar. I'll be staying here tonight and tomorrow, and then I'm going out to Arusha to meet some deads coming in for the hunting, and any time before then I'll do it for you if you say the word. Think about it. Will you think about it? Promise me that you'll think about it."

"I'll think about it," Klein said.

"Good. Good. Thank you. Now let's have lunch and change the subject. Do you like eating here?"

"One thing puzzles me. Why does this place have a clientele that's exclusively non-African? Does it dare to discriminate against blacks in a black republic?"

Gracchus laughed. "It's the blacks who discriminate, friend. This is considered a second-class hotel. All the blacks are at the Kilimanjaro or the Nyerere. Still, it's not such a bad place. I recommend the fish dishes, if you haven't tried them, and there's a decent white wine from Israel that—"

Eight

O Lord, methought what pain it was to drown!
What dreadful noise of water in mine ears!
What sights of ugly death within mine eyes!
Methoughts I saw a thousand fearful wracks;
A thousand men that fishes gnawed upon;
Wedges of gold, great anchors, heaps of pearl,
Inestimable stones, unvalued jewels,
All scatt'red in the bottom of the sea.
Some lay in dead men's skulls, and in the holes
Where eyes did once inhabit there were crept,
As 'twere in scorn of eyes, reflecting gems
That wooed the slimy bottom of the deep
And mocked the dead bones that lay scatt'red by.

Shakespeare: *Richard III*

"Israeli wine," Mick Dongan was saying. "Well, I'll try anything once, especially if there's some neat little irony attached to it. I mean, there we were in Egypt, in *Egypt*, at this fabulous dinner party in the hills at Luxor, and our host is a Saudi prince, no less, in full tribal costume right down to the sunglasses, and when they bring out the roast lamb he grins devilishly and says, 'Of course we could always drink Mouton-Rothschild, but I do happen to have a small stock of select Israeli wines in my cellar, and because I think you are, like myself, a connoisseur of small incongruities, I've asked my steward to open a bottle or two of'—Klein, do you see that girl who just came in?" It is January, 2021, early afternoon, a fine drizzle in the air. Klein is lunching with six colleagues from the history department at the Hanging Gardens atop the Westwood Plaza. The hotel is a huge ziggurat on stilts; the Hanging Gardens is a rooftop restaurant, ninety stories up, in freaky neo-Babylonian decor, all winged bulls and snorting dragons of blue and yellow tile, waiters with long curly beards and scimitars at their hips—gaudy nightclub by dark, campy faculty hangout by day. Klein looks to his left. Yes, a handsome woman, mid-twenties, coolly beautiful, serious-looking, taking a seat by herself, putting a stack of books and cassettes down on the table before her. Klein does not pick up strange girls: a matter of moral policy, and also a matter of innate shyness. Dongan teases him. "Go on over, will you? She's your type, I swear. Her eyes are the right color for you, aren't they?"

Klein has been complaining, lately, that there are too many blue-eyed gals in Southern California. Blue eyes are disturbing to him, somehow, even menacing. His own eyes are brown. So are hers: dark, warm, sparkling. He thinks he has seen her occasionally in the library. Perhaps they have even exchanged brief glances. "Go on," Dongan says. "Go on, Jorge. Go." Klein glares at him. He will not go. How can he intrude on this woman's privacy? To force himself on her—it would almost be like rape. Dongan smiles complacently; his bland grin is a merciless prod. Klein refuses to be stampeded. But then, as he hesitates, the girl smiles too, a quick shy smile, gone so soon he is not altogether sure it happened at all, but he is sure enough, and he finds himself rising, crossing the alabaster floor, hovering awkwardly over her, searching for some inspired words with which to make contact, and no words come, but still they make contact the old-fashioned way, eye to eye, and he is stunned by the intensity of what passes between them in that first implausible moment.

"Are you waiting for someone?" he mutters, shaken.

"No." The smile again, far less tentative. "Would you like to join me?"

She is a graduate student, he discovers quickly. Just got her master's, beginning now on her doctorate—the nineteenth-century East African slave trade, particular emphasis on Zanzibar. "How romantic," he says. "Zanzibar! Have you been there?"

"Never. I hope to go some day. Have you?"

"Not ever. But it always interested me, ever since I was a small boy collecting stamps. It was the last country in my album."

"Not in mine," she says. "Zululand was."

She knows him by name, it turns out. She had even been thinking of enrolling in his course on Nazism and Its Offspring. "Are you South American?" she asks.

"Born there. Raised here. My grandparents were East German. Grandfather was sent to Buenos Aires in '77 on a diplomatic mission and defected."

"Why Argentina? I thought that's been a hotbed of fascists since the old Nazi days."

"Was, yes. Was a long time ago. Also still full of German-speaking people, though. All their friends went there. But it was too unstable. My parents got out in '95, just before one of the big revolutions, and came to California. What about you?"

"British family. I was born in Seattle. My father's in the consular service. He—"

A waiter looms. They order sandwiches offhandedly. Lunch seems very unimportant now. The contact still holds. He sees Conrad's *Nostromo* in her stack of books; she is halfway through it, and he has just finished it, and the coincidence amuses them. Conrad is one of her favorites, she says. One of his, too. What about Faulkner? Yes, and Mann, and Virginia Woolf, and they share even a fondness for Hermann Broch, and a dislike for Hesse. How odd. Operas? *Freischütz, Holländer, Fidelio,* yes. "We have very Teutonic tastes," she observes.

"We have very similar tastes," he adds. He finds himself holding her hand.

"Amazingly similar," she says.

Mick Dongan leers at him from the far side of the room; Klein gives him a terrible scowl. Dongan winks. "Let's get out of here," Klein says, just as she starts to say the same thing.

They talk half the night and make love until dawn. "You ought to know," he tells her, solemnly over breakfast, "that I decided long ago never to get married and certainly never to have a child."

"So did I," she says. "When I was fifteen."

81

They were married four months later. Mick Dongan was his best man.

Gracchus said, as they left the restaurant, "You will think things over, won't you?"

"I will," Klein said. "I promised you that."

He went to his room, packed his suitcase, checked out, and took a cab to the airport, arriving in plenty of time for the afternoon flight to Zanzibar. The same melancholy little man was on duty as health officer when he landed, Barwani. "Sir, you have come back," Barwani said. "I thought you might. The other people have been here several days already."

"The other people?"

"When you were here last, sir, you kindly offered me a retainer in order that you might be informed when a certain person reached this island." Barwani's eyes gleamed. "That person, with two of her former companions, is here now."

Klein carefully placed a twenty-shilling note on the health officer's desk.

"At which hotel?"

Barwani's lips quirked. Evidently twenty shillings fell short of expectations. But Klein did not take out another banknote, and after a moment Barwani said, "As before. The Zanzibar House. And you, sir?"

"As before," Klein said. "I'll be staying at the Shirazi."

Sybille was in the garden of the hotel, going over that day's research notes, when the telephone call came from Barwani. "Don't let my papers blow away," she said to Zacharias, and went inside.

When she returned, looking bothered, Zacharias said, "Is there trouble?"

She sighed. "Jorge. He's on his way to his hotel now."

"What a bore," Mortimer murmured. "I thought Gracchus might have brought him to his senses."

"Evidently not," Sybille said. "What are we going to do?"

"What would you like to do?" Zacharias asked.

She shook her head. "We can't allow this to go on, can we?"

The evening air was humid and fragrant. The long rains had come and gone, and the island was in the grip of the new season's lunatic fertility: outside the window of Klein's hotel room some vast twining vine was putting forth monstrous trumpet-shaped yellow flowers, and all about the hotel grounds everything was in blossom, everything was in a frenzy of moist young leaves. Klein's sensibility reverberated to that feeling of universal vigorous thrusting newness; he paced the room, full of energy, trying to devise some feasible stratagem. Go immediately to see Sybille? Force his way in, if necessary, with shouts and alarums, and demand to know why she had told him that fantastic tale of imaginary sultans? No. No. He would do no more confronting, no more lamenting; now that he was here, now that he was close by her, he would seek her out calmly, he would talk quietly, he would invoke memories of their old love, he would speak of Rilke and Woolf and Broch, of afternoons in Puerto Vallarta and nights in Santa Fe, of music heard and caresses shared, he would rekindle not their marriage, for that was impossible, but merely the remembrance of the bond that once had existed, he would win from her some acknowledgment of what had been, and then he would soberly and quietly exorcise that bond, he and she together, they would work to free him by speaking softly of the change that had come over their lives, until, after three hours or four or five, he had brought himself with her help to an acceptance of the unacceptable. That was all. He would demand nothing, he would beg for nothing, except only that she assist him for one evening in ridding his soul of this useless, destructive obsession. Even a dead, even a capricious, wayward, volatile, whimsical, wanton dead, would surely see the desirability of that, and would freely give him her cooperation. Surely. And then home, and then new beginnings, too long postponed.

He made ready to go out.

There was a soft knock at the door. "Sir? Sir? You have visitors downstairs."

"Who?" Klein asked, though he knew the answer.

"A lady and two gentlemen," the bellhop replied. "The taxi has brought them from the Zanzibar House. They wait for you in the bar."

"Tell them I'll be down in a moment."

He went to the iced pitcher on the dresser, drank a glass of cold water mechanically, unthinkingly, poured himself a second, drained that too. This visit was unexpected; and why had she brought her entourage along? He had to struggle to regain that centeredness, that sense of purpose understood, which he thought he had attained before the knock. Eventually he left the room.

They were dressed crisply and impeccably this damp night, Zacharias in a tawny frock coat and pale-green trousers, Mortimer in a belted white caftan trimmed with intricate brocade, Sybille in a simple lavender tunic. Their pale faces were unmarred by perspiration; they seemed perfectly composed, models of poise. No one sat near them in the bar. As Klein entered, they stood to greet him, but their smiles appeared sinister, having nothing of friendliness in them. Klein clung tight to his intended calmness. He said quietly, "It was kind of you to come. May I buy drinks for you?"

"We have ours already," Zacharias pointed out. "Let us be your hosts. What will you have?"

"Pimm's Number Six," Klein said. He tried to match their frosty smiles. "I admire your tunic, Sybille. You all look so debonair tonight that I feel shamed."

"You never were famous for your clothes," she said.

Zacharias returned from the counter with Klein's drink. He took it and toasted them gravely.

After a short while Klein said, "Do you think I could talk privately with you, Sybille?"

"There's nothing we have to say to one another that can't be said in front of Kent and Laurence."

"Nevertheless."

"I prefer not to, Jorge."

"As you wish." Klein peered straight into her eyes and saw nothing there, nothing, and flinched. All that he had meant to say fled his mind. Only churning fragments danced there: Rilke, Broch, Puerto Vallarta. He gulped at his drink.

Zacharias said, "We have a problem to discuss, Klein."

84

"Go on."

"The problem is you. You're causing great distress to Sybille. This is the second time, now, that you've followed her to Zanzibar, to the literal end of the earth, Klein, and you've made several attempts besides to enter a closed sanctuary in Utah under false pretenses, and this is interfering with Sybille's freedom, Klein, it's an impossible, intolerable interference."

"The deads are dead," Mortimer said. "We understand the depths of your feelings for your late wife, but this compulsive pursuit of her must be brought to an end."

"It will be," Klein said, staring at a point on the stucco wall midway between Zacharias and Sybille. "I want only an hour or two of private conversation with my—with Sybille, and then I promise you that there will be no further—"

"Just as you promised Anthony Gracchus," Mortimer said, "not to go to Zanzibar."

"I wanted—"

"We have our rights," said Zacharias. "We've gone through hell, literally through hell, to get where we are. You've infringed on our right to be left alone. You bother us. You bore us. You annoy us. We hate to be annoyed." He looked toward Sybille. She nodded. Zacharias' hand vanished into the breast pocket of his coat. Mortimer seized Klein's wrist with astonishing suddenness and jerked his arm forward. A minute metal tube glistened in Zacharias' huge fist. Klein had seen such a tube in the hand of Anthony Gracchus only the day before.

"No," Klein gasped. "I don't believe—*no!*"

Zacharias plunged the cold tip of the tube quickly into Klein's forearm.

"The freezer unit is coming," Mortimer said. "It'll be here in five minutes or less."

"What if it's late?" Sybille asked anxiously. "What if something irreversible happens to his brain before it gets here?"

"He's not even entirely dead yet," Zacharias reminded her. "There's time. There's ample time. I spoke to the doctor myself, a very intelligent Chinese, flawless command of English. He was most sympathetic. They'll have him frozen within a couple minutes of death. We'll book cargo passage aboard the morning plane for Dar. He'll be in the United States within twenty-four hours, I guarantee that. San Diego will be notified. Everything will be all right, Sybille!"

Jorge Klein lay slumped across the table. The bar had emptied the moment he had cried out and lurched forward: the half-dozen customers had fled, not caring to mar their holidays by sharing an evening with the presence of death, and the waiters and bartenders, big-eyed, terrified, lurked in the hallway. A heart attack, Zacharias had announced, some kind of sudden attack, maybe a stroke, where's the telephone? No one had seen the tiny tube do its work.

Sybille trembled. "If anything goes wrong—"

"I hear the sirens now," Zacharias said.

From his desk at the airport Daud Mahmoud Barwani watched the bulky refrigerated coffin being loaded by grunting porters aboard the morning plane for Dar. And then, and then, and then? They would ship the dead man to the far side of the world, to America, and breathe new life into him, and he would go once more among men. Barwani shook his head. These people! The man who was alive is now dead, and these dead ones, who knows what they are? Who knows? Best that the dead remain dead, as was intended in the time of first things. Who could have foreseen a day when the dead returned from the grave? Not I. And who can foresee what we will all become, a hundred years from now? Not I. Not I. A hundred years from now I will sleep, Barwani thought. I will sleep, and it will not matter to me at all what sort of creatures walk the earth.

Nine

We die with the dying:
See, they depart, and we go with them.
We are born with the dead:
See, they return, and bring us with them.

T.S. Eliot: *Little Gidding*

On the day of his awakening he saw no one except the attendants at the rekindling house, who bathed him and fed him and helped him to walk slowly around his room. They said nothing to him, nor he to them; words seemed irrelevant. He felt strange in his skin, too snugly contained, as though all his life he had worn ill-fitting clothes and now had for the first time encountered a competent tailor. The images that his eyes brought him were sharp, unnaturally clear, and faintly haloed by prismatic colors, an effect that imperceptibly vanished as the day passed. On the second day he was visited by the San Diego Guidefather, not at all the formidable patriarch he had imagined, but rather a cool, efficient executive, about fifty years old, who greeted him cordially and told him briefly of the disciplines and routines he must master before he could leave the Cold Town. "What month is this?" Klein asked, and Guidefather told him it was June, the seventeenth of June, 2033. He had slept four weeks.

Now it is the morning of the third day after his awakening, and he has guests: Sybille, Nerita, Zacharias, Mortimer, Gracchus. They file into his room and stand in an arc at the foot of his bed, radiant in the glow of light that pierces the narrow windows. Like demigods, like angels, glittering with a dazzling inward brilliance, and now he is of their company. Formally they embrace him, first Gracchus, then Nerita, then Mortimer. Zacharias advances next to his bedside, Zacharias who sent him into death, and he smiles at Klein and Klein returns the smile, and they embrace. Then it is Sybille's turn: she slips her hand between his, he draws her close, her lips brush his cheek, his touch hers, his arm encircles her shoulders.

"Hello," she whispers.

"Hello," he says.

They ask him how he feels, how quickly his strength is returning, whether he has been out of bed yet, how soon he will commence his drying-off. The style of their conversation is the oblique, elliptical style favored by the deads, but not nearly so clipped and cryptic as the way of speech they normally would use among themselves; they are favoring him, leading him inch by inch into their customs. Within five minutes he thinks he is getting the knack.

He says, using their verbal shorthand, "I must have been a great burden to you."

"You were, you were," Zacharias agrees. "But all that is done with now."

"We forgive you," Mortimer says.

"We welcome you among us," declares Sybille.

They talk about their plans for the months ahead. Sybille is nearly finished with her work on Zanzibar; she will retreat to Zion Cold Town for the summer months to write her thesis. Mortimer and Nerita are off to Mexico to tour the ancient temples and pyramids; Zacharias is going to Ohio, to his beloved mounds. In the autumn they will reassemble at Zion and plan the winter's amusement: a tour of Egypt, perhaps, or Peru, the heights of Machu Picchu. Ruins, archaeological sites, delight them; in the places where death has been busiest, their joy is most intense. They are flushed, excited, verbose— virtually chattering, now. Away we will go, to Zimbabwe, to Palenque, to Angkor, to Knossos, to Uxmal, to Nineveh, to Mohenjo-daro. And as they go on and on, talking with hands and eyes and smiles and even words, even words, torrents of words, they blur and become unreal to him, they are mere dancing puppets jerking about a badly painted stage, they are droning insects, wasps or bees or mosquitoes, with all their talk of travels and festivals, of Boghazköy and Babylon, of Megiddo and Masada, and he ceases to hear them, he tunes them out, he lies there smiling, eyes glazed, mind adrift. It perplexes him that he has so little interest in them. But then he realizes that it is a mark of his liberation. He is freed of old chains now. Will he join their set? Why should he? Perhaps he will travel with them, perhaps not, as the whim takes him. More likely not. Almost certainly not. He does not need their company. He has his own interests. He will follow Sybille about no longer. He does not need, he does not want, he will not seek. Why should he become one of them, rootless, an amoral wanderer, a ghost made flesh? Why should he embrace the values and customs of these people who had given him to death as dispassionately as they might swat an insect, only because he had bored them, because he had annoyed them? He does not hate them for what they did to him, he feels no resentment that he can identify, he merely chooses to detach himself from them. Let them float on from ruin to ruin, let them pursue death from continent to continent; he will go his own way. Now that he has crossed the interface, he finds that Sybille no longer matters to him.

—*Oh, sir, things change*—

"We'll go now," Sybille says softly.

He nods. He makes no other reply.

"We'll see you after your drying-off," Zacharias tells him, and touches him lightly with his knuckles, a farewell gesture used only by the deads.

"See you," Mortimer says.

"See you," says Gracchus.

"Soon," Nerita says.

Never, Klein says, saying it without words, but so they will understand. Never. Never. Never. I will never see any of you. I will never see you, Sybille. The syllables echo through his brain, and the word, *never, never, never,* rolls over him like the breaking surf, cleansing him, purifying him, healing him. He is free. He is alone.

"Goodbye," Sybille calls from the hallway.

"Goodbye," he says.

It was years before he saw her again. But they spent the last days of '39 together, shooting dodos under the shadow of mighty Kilimanjaro.

PART TWO:

QUICKEN

DAMIEN
BRODERICK

One

90 I am called Dr. Imam Hassan Sabbāh," said the man in the Islamic skullcap, a white embroidered taqiyah. "You may address me as Guidefather, Professor Klein."

Klein uttered the vocable denoting "Thank you, sir" in the register of submission. Even now, after these months as a dead, he remained surprised by his fluency in the swift argot shared by his postmortem fellows. Had he learned it, in the way children acquire a vernacular, simply by interacting with other deads, being in their midst, listening to their conversation, climbing a ladder from baby-simple to adult-complexified? No. After an initial week or two of confusion and difficulty in San Diego Cold Town, the new language had emerged spontaneously from his lips, driven presumably by some immense rearrangement of grammar and lexicon from Spanish, English, German, French, his linguistic X-bar trees. All that apparatus of speech and thought tucked away inside the folds of his revived brain. But when had it occurred, this Rosetta Stone of the reborn, this downloaded Berlitz course? He assumed it must have been a side effect of rekindling, or perhaps (was this too paranoiac?) it had been literally stamped upon his vulnerable defunct cortex during the four unconscious weeks in suspension and repair following his death. All he knew for sure was that he and this Muslim Guidefather were equally glib in their accelerated and concise tongue.

"I am here at the invitation of your staff, but nothing has been explained," he added. "How may I serve the Conclave?" Five tonal phonemes. However it had been done, it was an impressive accomplishment.

"You are a gifted man, Jorge. It seems that you resist the temptation of ennui, cafard, the sport of absurdity, indulgence in the iconography of mortality."

"A temptation gladly acceded to by my wife Sybille," Klein said, bored by the words even as he spoke. No resentment. It was as remarkable, in its way, as his magical acquisition of the music of the dead. Had they rewired his amygdala, his emotional keyboard, his flux of neurotransmitters? No doubt, but Klein knew himself the merest amateur in the sciences of cognition and neurology. Such speculations were useless, then, as well as dull. Still, some small part of his well-trained mind gnawed at the question and its implications. He could not be bothered trying to still it.

"Your *ex*-wife," said the Guidefather. A sharp one syllable rebuke. You have been here long enough to know better than that, Klein, the man did not need to say.

"Yes, yes. All bonds broken, I am fully aware of this. Perhaps I resent her flight from all responsibility." The words clattered in his mouth. Really, he didn't care what Sybille did. His obsession with her was expunged, their obliterated decade, their lost Jorge-and-Sybille. Wasn't it?

"The transition of the rekindled leaves us stranded in absurdity," Sabbāh said, as if it were an admission. Klein watched him, surprised. The man's hands lay flat on his thighs; his mouth, through the beard and mustache, suggested a restrained amusement. "Yet we have built the Cold Towns from nothing, we conduct our battles with the pests of the Treasury and Internal Revenue, we pursue our research and marketing. We are not monks, withdrawn from the world, even when we withdraw from the world into our sanctuaries. You follow me."

"I believe so. You hope to enlist me as...how should I put it... middle management."

Sabbāh smiled. "Not quite, Professor. As an emissary, eventually. For now, as an Acolyte. Better yet, an Adjutant. The Conclave wishes you to reenter the world of the warms and learn in detail how we are regarded. What risks we face. How we might best advance our cause and pursue our goals."

Do not ask direct questions, Klein recalled. Dolorosa's advice, that shabby outcast. Still, though that edict now seemed entirely natural and proper, he forced himself.

"And what are those goals, Guidefather?"

"You will learn this in good time." The man rose, made no attempt to take Jorge Klein's hand. "That will be all for now. We shall dine this evening in the Rojo Diablo restaurant at eight. You will be prompt."

Irritated, Klein remained seated. "You presume too easily, Guidefather."

"You were dead, now you walk. Payment is due to your fellows."

"My insurance covered your hefty fee for my rekindling. For my ex-wife's also. Now the Conclave holds attached all my assets—my property, my savings, my future income. You can ask no more."

Hassan Sabbāh walked to the door, opened it, stood waiting for Klein to rise.

"You have paid in the currency of the living," he said. "Now we seek your cooperation, freely given. Nothing will be forced or extorted. Good morning, Dr. Klein. I shall see you tonight."

"Very well," Klein said, and rose. He followed Sabbāh into the dreary, unornamented hallway. In silence, they parted at an intersection and he made his way to his simple room. His breathing remained calm, the infusion of respirocytes flooded through his vascular system carrying oxygen to his renovated and reconstructed brain, along with its unknown cargo of neuromodulators. You are dead, he thought. And now you walk. You are without family or spouse, except for this company of the deceased. Yes, your parents remain alive, and your sister Hester, and your cousins in America and Argentina, but to them you are truly dead. They have sat *shiva* for seven days in your memory, and now to them you are as good as buried, alive only in their memories—memories poisoned by your apostasy from the world of the warms. He went into his room and lay down on the simple bed, eyes open, gazing at the plastic meaninglessness of the world.

* * *

Rolling Stone's *I See Dead People 101*

I've never seen any deads younger than maybe 20, or older than 50 or 60. What's up with that?

Maybe it's built into the process (whatever that is). As usual, the Conclave of the Rekindled refuse to divulge any details, but top gerontologists and neuroscientists suggest that rekindling a postmortem child would, like, upset the balance of the universe—or at least mess with the kid's developmental trajectory.

And maybe old people are too far gone. The deads are probably working on it in their labs. If they have labs.

How that kid thing would cash out is anyone's guess. Maybe the Cold Towns have special schools or dormitories for the, you know, differently dead. It doesn't sound like a lot of fun to be stuck at the size and age of six years old for the rest of eternity, or even for a few thousand years. (Nobody yet knows how long the dead will stay… well, "alive" isn't the right word. Active. Ambulant. Not-really-dead.)

Is it true that after they dry off, deads are gifted with a pile of gold equal to their weight?

Let us reason together. Suppose the average American adult weighs 180 lbs. Yes, that's an understatement and has been for decades, but the Grim Reset probably carved quite a bit of flab off of a lot of citizens. 180 lbs. is 2,880 ounces (31.1034768 grams to the Troy ounce, since you ask), and today's gold fix is $New17.67 per ounce. That'd be more than 50,000 Newbucks per dead, on average. Readers who remember the Bad Old Days probably still recalibrate that as five million USD. Per person.

How likely is that? Rounding off, we have 500 million citizens in the USA, more than half in the prime adult catchment area (like, not kids or olds). But not so many of those 280-Megs die and get rekindled—statisticians estimate about point one percent, and that's as fine-toothed as it gets, because the Census doesn't count dead people. They're dead, right?

Still, that's maybe two hundred and fifty thousand humans eligible to stick their demortified paws out for their gratuity once they die. More than a trillion old USD/10 billion Newbucks. And where is that absurd pile of loot supposed to come from?

Mark this one: *Urban Legend.*

So who does fund the Cold Towns? Those things are spreading like toadstools after a clammy rain. And now they're even taking over prime real estate in our city. Why, the ancient cathedral of—

Calm down. People live where they like, especially when they can afford the real estate. You want to set up ghettoes? Get out of here!

Call it communism, if you like; call it Galt's Gulch meets Valentine Michael Smith. (You're *au fait* of the classics, right? No? Hit the download. We'll be here when you get back.) As far as we can tell—locked out here on the wrong side of their guarded gates—it looks as if the deads share their wealth in an egalitarian way that demands only as much in way of toil as each rekindled is prepared to offer. Machine service to the max.

Most of their community funding comes, of course, from their fabulous patents. Who did you suppose collects the dues for your household cool fusion power system, or the Paycell in your finger? The deads are different from you and me, Scott. They're smarter. And they're richer.

Two

Barn's burnt down —
now
I can see the moon.

Mizuta Masahide (1657–1723)

Sylvie, the young departmental manager, offered Klein a comfortable enough armchair in a nicely appointed anteroom off the large sixth floor Bunche Hall office currently occupied by Professor Bik Liu, Chair of UCLA's Department of History. *Verboten* to grad students and lesser creatures, this was the parking station, Klein reflected, for Business and First Class academics. Sylvie tapped, offered him coffee and a slice of her chocolate birthday cake, which he declined. She flushed, presumably dreading a *faux pas*, and retreated behind her systems display.

Klein examined the two familiar duck-hunting prints and one rather Lucian Freudish daubing—all grim mustards and murky khakis and shit-browns—of what he supposed was an American tourist couple gazing up at the ceiling of the Sistine Chapel. His lips quirked. The heavy quake-proof door opened, and Bik ushered him into her spacious sanctum, shook his hand with only minimal squeamishness, sat him in a less comfortable chair beside the mandatory wall of old books and journals, antique archival image of itself in an epoch of information storage at the scale of electrons and qubits. Hot afternoon Los Angeles light filtered through the wide solar screened windows. Plainly Bik was flustered, and she was never flustered.

"Jorge, you look well," she said, and then bit her lip. Gaunt, deliberately gray haired, she was a decade older than Klein, and looked closer to twice that.

"For a dead guy," Klein said.

Bik colored slightly, a Lucian Freudish color. She ruled her domain with iron and sound judgment, but this was an intrusion from beyond the grave. Klein had to remind himself how few American warms ever met a dead.

"No need to lie about *my* looking well," she said. "I look like something the *chat* dragged in. Or the *chienne*."

He watched her eyes. She was a clown, he was a clown, all the world was a pointless pratfall into mud. China had no cats, he recalled, not any longer, even with the cornucopia that had followed upon the cool fusion rollout half a decade ago. Not many dogs, either.

"Well. I dare say you've been traveling?" Bik said.

"Yes, visiting the Cold Towns." Without changing his tone, Klein said, "You want me out, I take it?"

She cleared her throat. "You are more direct than I recall."

"We are less concerned with the niceties," he told her, "we deads. I understand you've had some difficulties yourself. I hope everything turned out well?" He had done his due diligence; Bik had suffered a serious cardiac attack six months earlier, and now had a new heart. The experience had diminished her.

"Not a big deal, Jorge. Autologous regrowth, no need for a transplant. So I suppose in a way we've been through the same wars."

"Actually, no," he said. "Not really."

After a silence, she said carefully, "You understand why I asked you to drop in today. I am regretful for the necessity, but the institutional governance—"

"I have no objection to forced retirement, but I do expect the department to allow me the privileges and status of professor emeritus."

"That can certainly be arranged. The university board has proposed a new title for rekindled scholars of your standing, Jorge."

"Yes. Professor mortuus." He showed his teeth. "I can live with that."

Again, a faint quiver in her surgically tightened upper eyelids, and a tight smile. "Very good. Do you still drink spirits, Jorge?"

"Of course. We eat, we drink, we sleep, we dream, I'm sure you've read the Sunday supplements. Some aspects of life we have put behind us, or are closed to our condition, but fortunately a good whiskey is not one of them."

Golden fluid caught a ray of light, swirled in the glass she handed him. Bik sipped her own. "You mean to continue your researches?"

"Into the Nazi epoch, the *Konzentrationslager*? Buchenwald, Dachau, Auschwitz-Birkenau? The millions murdered with no rekindling? No. I'm done with that. But what I am is a professor of contemporary history, Bik, and contemporary history is what has remade me in its likeness. Mortuus." He tasted the scotch. He might have been drinking turpentine. He put the glass on her desk and rose. "I shall study the deads. In due course, I shall lecture to your students on the topic."

At the door she took his hand again, and held it loosely. "I'm very pleased that we shan't lose you entirely, Jorge, and I speak personally as well as for the whole department. Give my love to—" She faltered again, and now her face took on an ashen tint. "I'm sorry. I'm sorry. But you do still see…" She broke off.

"Sybille? Rarely, Bik. Matthew, chapter 22, verse 30."

"Understood." She recited it from memory, as he'd known she would. Bik was not a woman of piety, not even a Christian, but this verse was now inscribed in the shell-shocked consciousness of the world of the warms. The intellectual warms, at least. O my prophetic soul. "For when the dead rise, they will neither marry nor be given in marriage. In this respect they will be like the angels in heaven.'"

"Just so. Like an angel, Professor. Like an angel."

The young manager was waiting for him as he left the Chair's office. Her blouse, his sharp eyes noticed, was now unsealed at her sternum, open enough to show off a substantial portion of her golden brown breasts, their deep cleavage. Something avid in her gaze.

"Professor Klein—" she began, broke off. "I took your course on the rise of the Third Reich, five years ago. You won't remember."

He didn't. He regarded her coolly. She was breathing faster. Not fear of *faux pas*, then, as he'd supposed earlier, but some sort of perverse appetite?

"Of course I remember you. Sylvie, isn't it?"

She smiled, still nervous, but there was a bold amusement in her gaze. "I thought you were wonderful. I always had a...well, a crush. And then I heard you'd been rekindled." She turned away from him, looking back over her shoulder, checking the Chair's closed door, and back to Klein. "Have you ever played the President and the Temptress? Everyone's watching the series on stereo." And to Jorge Klein's astonishment, she leaned across her desk, took the hem of her skirt in both hands, and flipped it up. Her buttocks were round and smooth, divided by a startlingly crimson thong. Sylvie let the skirt fall, turning, and took up something long and leaf-brown from the desk. She proffered it. "We could go to Andrew Sinclair's office, he's away at the Aung San Suu Kyi colloquium."

No faintest stirring in his prick, no tightening of his balls. He looked back at her dispassionately, with just a touch of amusement. Slick Willy and Monica, eh? The uses of history.

"I'm sorry, Sylvie," he said.

She flushed again, licked her mouth, shook her head.

"I'm sorry, too, Professor Klein. I misunderstood. Please don't tell—"

"My lips," he said, "are sealed."

"Oh my god, I've made such a fool of myself."

"Not your fault, mine entirely. We are wondrously changed, we deads, and not always in a good way. Anyway, take your consolation from what old father Freud taught us."

Her flush had receded. She put the panatela back on the desk.

"Superego *uber alles?*"

"That too," he said, amused. "No, Sigmund offered a more specific and relevant piece of advice. Sometimes a cigar is just a cigar."

The lovely young woman laughed loudly, and as she saw him out to the corridor pressed his hand. He felt nothing, nothing, nothing.

Three

There is no other God beside me; I kill and I make alive; I wound and I heal.

Deuteronomy. 32:39

De damnandis blaspheme redanimatisque

Papal Bull on the Condemnation and Excommunication of all blasphemous Heretics, known as the Conclave of the Rekindled, January 3, 2031.

Preamble

Of the damnable and blasphemously revivified, we proclaim our Condemnation.

Through the power given him from God, the Roman Pontiff has been appointed to administer spiritual and temporal punishments as each case severally deserves. The purpose of this is the repression of the wicked designs of misguided men, who have been so captivated by the debased impulse of their evil purposes as to forget the fear of the Lord, to set aside with contempt canonical decrees and apostolic commandments, and to dare to formulate new and false dogmas of sacred life and death, and to introduce the evil of "rebirth" after physical death—or to support, help and adhere to such lost souls, who make it their business to cleave asunder the seamless robe of our Redeemer and the unity of the orthodox faith. Hence it befits the Pontiff, lest the vessel of Peter appear to sail without pilot or oarsman, to take severe measures against such men and their followers, and by multiplying punitive measures and by other suitable remedies to see to it that these same overbearing men, devoted as they are to purposes of evil, along with their adherents, should not deceive the multitude of the simple by their lies and their deceitful devices, nor drag them along to share their own error and ruination, contaminating them with what amounts to a contagious disease, one far more terrible than death itself. It also befits the Pontiff, having condemned the "rekindled," to ensure their still greater confounding by publicly showing and openly declaring to all faithful Christians how formidable are the censures and punishments to which such guilt can lead; to the end that by such public declaration they themselves may return, in confusion and remorse, to their true deaths, making an unqualified withdrawal from the prohibited abomination; by this means they may escape divine vengeance and any degree of participation in their eternal damnation.

Fatwa against the so-called "Rekindled"

The revival of dead human beings, in a mockery of Allah's gift of life to the faithful, is against Islam, against the Prophet of Islam, and against the Koran. All those, alive and dead, who assist in this wicked endeavor, are condemned to capital punishment. I call on all valiant Muslims wherever they may be in the world to execute this sentence without delay, so that no one henceforth will dare insult and contravene the sacred teachings of the Prophet.

Concussion slapped Sybille awake. She stared in the darkness of the windowless room. The lighted clock display had gone black. No whisper of air-conditioning. A rushing, as of a great wind, and crackling roars, gusts, bangs. Voices cried out. Her chest hurt. Smoke. Another immense crash. High pitched bleating, on and on. My god, she thought. Zion Cold Town is on fire.

"Get on the floor," she said in two sharp syllables. Rolling across the wide bed, she found Kent Zacharias. He lay unmoving. The long-dead were hard to wake, she had noticed that more than once.

103

Groping in the darkness, she found his face, his nose, grasped it hard and twisted. Like a drowning man surfacing, Zacharias snorted and gasped.

"Sybille. Are we under attack?"

A stench of burning plastic-coated wiring, paint, probably clothing and furniture, other flammable stuff choked her throat.

"Out," she said. "Come on."

At the door, she banged her bare hip on the door knob. She pressed the back of her hand to the wood. It was distinctly warm, but not yet hot. Perhaps the fire was contained in the north wing, where public access was easier and the tall plate-glass windows would shatter in the boiling gases of a bomb. Smoke was the immediate hazard, poisonous and blinding. She opened the door a crack. Zacharias bumped her from behind, a large blundering animal.

"Don't open the damned door," he said, voice rasping.

"I have to, Kent," she told him. "We'll roast alive if we stay here." She flung it wide. Smoke poured in from the corridor, and a red and white glare danced in it. The floor was hot. "Put your shoes on," she said, and ran back bare-soled to her side of the bed and found her slippers. Naked, then, she returned to the corridor and turned left. Someone had a flashlight, and called, "This way." Other people were emerging from their rooms, moving in both directions, stumbling into each other.

Sybille raised her voice above the racket of the fire alarms. "Head for the back stairs. Down, not up." The milling took on an abrupt sense of purpose. "Has anyone called 911?"

"Not answering." A man's gruff tones. "Signal's jammed, or they're overloaded."

The stairwell door opened into emergency lights in a haze of smog. The lights immediately flickered and went out.

"Shit," someone said. "Listen up, people. Stay as low as you can. Crawl on your hands and knees if you have to. Try not to breathe this filthy stuff."

Like a procession of pilgrims in the dark night of the soul, they crawled and bumped and squirmed down the stairs, sweat pouring from their changed flesh, no more adroit or invulnerable under this threat of final death, Sybille thought madly, than any living creature fleeing in a forest fire. Crackling and crashing. The emergency door opened into cooler night, desert air. She fell through it. The flashlight was casting about, sweeping across the smeared, blackened faces of the dead. In the distance, another explosion slapped the air. The cinderblock walls remained untouched. Sybille thought: Is this why the architects chose these unpromising materials? She had supposed it was a statement against the vanity of the warms. *I have looked into the abyss*, the walls of the Cold Towns said bleakly, *and the abyss has looked back*. Well, this time the abyss had done a serviceable job. But next time we'd better find an improved method of lighting the damned place during assault.

Zacharias found her. To her astonishment, in the dimness, he wore a fire-retardant sheet like a silvery burqa. Where had he found that? Where had he managed to find the time to look for it? He took it off, gallant as Lord Raleigh and, hairy and naked, wrapped it around her own nakedness. It was cold and clammy.

"We can escape into the woods and then the desert," he said in her ear, "or go to the front and see what we can do to help."

"This place is ours," she said fiercely, hugging herself, starting to tremor. "Those sons of bitches—" The screams had subsided, but people were weeping. We dead spill our tears, she thought, even if our blood is thick with small machines. She heard no further sounds of explosions, but the rasping noise of flames grew louder by the moment.

"The fire will put itself out," Zacharias said. "There's really not that much to burn." He paused. "Your cassettes. Are they tucked away in a secure safe?"

"I think so," she told him. "Maybe one still in the machine. God *damn* it, where am I going to find another cassette player?" More than a decade earlier, the university had scoured the net markets for weeks before they turned up an antique Sony sound cassette player so she could transcribe the priceless, irreplaceable ethnographic interviews from Zanzibar. And now that machine was probably warped and melted, along with one of the tapes, charred into meaninglessness. Well, she thought. All right. This is the condition of the deads. Let the dead bury their dead. She shook her head, then, in self-rebuke. No. That was the apologist cant of those who yearned for death, proclaimed its virtue and necessity—the kinds of fools and bigots who had done this terrible thing.

"The fatwa," Zacharias said, echoing her thoughts. "Or that Bull of Pope Sixtus VII. The denunciations from the Russian Orthodox prelates. We were right to withdraw from them. We should cut off their cool fusion generators. Damn them to the Fifth Circle of Hell."

They had reached the front drive and forecourt of the building, and searchlights were blooming like flowers of cold fire, reflecting from the blurred crimson fire trucks that had finally arrived. Hard streams of water fell through the smoke, spitting in the gaping ruin of the building's entranceway. Amid the haze and hot sparks she saw another display of sparks, darting, purposeful, a swarm of stereo drones. From Zion's own media center, she suspected, or maybe Vox News was already on the scene. And yes, all the windows were shattered and gone, and the tall steel main doors lay buckled and useless. Bodies were being borne out on floating stretchers, ready for the retrieval ambulances. Perhaps they could be saved. The deads, Sybille told herself grimly, are hard to kill. She walked forward into the ruin, in her silver mortuary robe like the white-wrapped figure from Arnold Böcklin's painting *Die Toteninsel*, drifting across dark water to the embrace of the Isle of the Dead, and felt almost nothing but brief surprise when the whole tall wall, tormented by flame, explosive shock, and the pounding of the hose, fell upon her, sundering her spine in a burst of agony, smashing her legs and hips. The drones, the media flies and bees, surrounded her, hungrily, like tiny metallic and crystal carrion eaters. For a second time Sybille Klein died.

The phone implant buzzed against the back of his ear, waking Klein instantly. "What time is it?"

"4:32 a.m., Professor Klein, September 29, 2037," the machine said. "You have two urgent calls."

"From?"

"One is from your Guidefather, Dr. Hassan Sabbāh. The other is from your sister, Hester Solom—"

"Hester?" he said, in disbelief. "At four in the morning?"

"She is in London. Do you wish to take her call?"

"Very well. Put her through. If the call takes longer than two minutes, place her on hold and let me speak to the Imam."

"I have your brother now, Mrs. Solomon."

"Jorge?" The woman's voice, so like his mother's, was frantic.

"What's the matter, Hester? Is it father?"

"What? No, no, we're all fine. Not that you'd care." The inevitable touch of bitterness. He'd scarcely seen any of them since his marriage, not even during the bereavement service for his dead wife. "Look, turn on your stereo. Vox News."

"I never watch that crap." He threw his legs over the sides of the bed, felt around in the dim light of the utilities for his slippers. "What is it? The Second Coming of Jesus?"

"Just turn the goddamned thing on."

The stereopsis TV frame deepened as he spoke the command, and switched directly to a scene of smoke, white-hot fire, shouting men in protective suits and helmets, contained chaos. A Cold Town, evidently. Yes, a bright blue line of text ran across the depth display like a message from the impalpable Hand of Yahweh. *Bombing at Zion Cold Town. Seven deads defuncted at least 13 badly damaged.*

His pulse increased a fraction, and he was aware of a pulsing in his temples. The New Man has not entirely displaced the Old Man, he thought.

"Do you see her?" Hester was wailing. "Did you see Sybille?"

Images cascaded, jump cuts, paired hologramic bugs seeking the most striking and disturbing pictures. Yes, there she was, crushed under a fall of broken cinderblock. In the tank, her face loomed. Still the same pale, beautiful Michelangelo marble as the moment she'd died the first time, despite the streaks of grime. A revival team was struggling with the hill of broken masonry. In the background, flames were abating, driven back by the foam and water. The image cut away, and again, and again. His accelerated rekindled thoughts slowed into a sort of paralysis. Not so *over her* after all, part of his consciousness observed sardonically. A world without meaning meant, surely, that a doubled death of a woman once loved ardently, desperately, obsessionally was without meaning. But no. Not quite. Not at all, in fact.

This is an aberration, he told himself. I will recover my poise in a moment. Besides, the black cryo van is pulling up now, I imagine, and they will have her ruined body in the repair shop within minutes. She's right there in the very heart of a major Cold Town, he thought. No better location if someone's going to kill you.

"Dr. Klein," said a deep voice, barely accented.

Hassan Sabbāh. "Yes, Guidefather," Klein said. "My sister just called to tell me that Sybille—"

"She will be rekindled," Sabbāh told him patiently. "In fact, this is why I am calling you. We have decided to advance your position with the Conclave. There are aspects of the revivified you must witness, if you are to act as our speaker among the living."

"Your speak—"

"Get dressed in warm clothes and meet me in the quad. We have a fusion aircraft on standby. You will be with your ex-wife within two hours." He broke contact. Hester's voice came back, high pitched, aghast. Perhaps she had not even noticed his absence.

"I have to go, dear sister," he told her. "They are flying me to Utah. I'll catch up with you and the parents as soon as I can." He heard a gasp. "I know," he said with an edge in his voice, "'What do you have to *do* around here to get some attention, *die* or something?' Apparently so. Good night."

He dressed snugly and went outside into the cool morning, still sunless, harshly lit by the exterior LEDs. Guidefather stood beside the open passenger hatch of a small Gates fusion jet, a couple of functionaries in attendance. Klein climbed aboard, strapped in, and within a minute was hurtling toward his defuncted wife. Ex-wife.

Four

Human life, because it is marked by a beginning and an end, becomes whole, an entity in itself that can be subjected to judgment, only when it has ended in death; death not merely ends life, it also bestows upon it a silent completeness, snatched from the hazardous flux to which all things human are subject.

Hannah Arendt, *The Life of the Mind*

Hard blue-white lighting, sterility itself, diagnostic and monitoring equipment gleaming, the large tank waiting for its occupant, and Sybille supine on a gurney, motionless, eyes shut, totally hairless after the ministrations of the techs, her round scalp eerily pale above her faintly tanned features, breasts flattened only slightly by gravity, the curved purse of her vulva visible within the torn flesh and sundered bone of her smashed hips, legs so badly broken they seemed the remnants of a carnivore's meal. He had not seen her for four years, and this broken corpse was no memory of his.

"You're going to amputate her limbs," Klein conjectured. He stood beside the gurney with Zion's Guidefather, a purple-skinned fellow as ruthlessly shaved as Sybille. A former Marine? A Navy SEAL? Both wore transparent, flexible outer shell and helmet over decontaminated scrubs, in common with the handful of busy medical technicians, all of them, unsurprisingly, deads. The hiss of air from sealed tanks, a faint echo in the voice circuits.

"Nothing so gross. You are here to witness the restoration process, or at least its first steps. Watch in silence."

Sybille's corpse was lifted into the tank, lowered on a mesh into some viscous, transparent medium. She—it—seemed to float, rolling slightly, was stabilized by mesh from above. Tubes extruded from the sides of the tank, sharp-tipped; they entered her flesh. After a long minute, her skin took on a roseate flush.

"Repair nanocytes," said the Guidefather, Jamal Hakim. "This much the academics and media of the warms have long conjectured. But wait."

The corpse began to swell. Pulsations flexed Sybille's smashed legs, her hips writhed in a horrid parody of sexual desire. Klein watched without emotion, neither excited nor repelled. The world was comic in its meaningless surges, its appetites, its agonies, but none of what he saw brought a smile to his lips or a burning wish to vomit. Awareness of his own inanition caused him neither self-reproof nor an anxious wish to remedy this loss of emotions that had once overwhelmed his life. All of this he saw clearly, layer within layer, and all he felt was a profound bleakness.

A deep thrumming, and the lights flickered. Magnetic forces, no doubt, the kind of sleeting impalpable magic wrought by resonance scanners. So this is why they insisted we remove all metal from our bodies, change into these scrubs and booties. Even the tanks of air on our backs must be ceramic or plastic. The techs watched their instruments, the dead woman's body swelled, ballooned, limbs straightening under some impulse he could not detect except through its effects.

"We have engaged her morphogenetic *Bauplan* field," Hakim said. His deep voice was a profound baritone, effortlessly piercing the rumble of the hidden magnetrons within the tank, in the majestic tones of a cantor in Temple, a holy, authoritative growl of absolute precision. Klein caught himself. Holy? Such nonsense. This place was no more than a highly elaborate body works, a repair shop.

"Body plan," Klein glossed aloud. "Some genetic master code, I take it."

"In part. But rekindling searches the genomic recipes in a large sampling of healthy cells of the body, under the direction of the morphic field, and recovers a pristine image of the epigenetic landscape and that maximal state toward which it moves."

Gibberish, surely. This was the kind of nonsense peddled in the lower echelons of the media. *The Grays Walk Among Us. Christian Crystal Therapy. Nazi Deads Secret Bases on the Backside of the Moon.*

He had sampled them in his studies, when he lived, at first amused, finally infuriated and even sickened by the malign know-nothing gullibility they stood for. Could the Guidefather be pranking him? Testing him in an obscure rite, probing at his own vulnerability to such drivel? It seemed impossible. It was impossible.

"I'm sorry, sir, I can't understand how the information inside widely separated and differentiated cells could—"

"Quantum entanglement. We are bathing the defuncted body with powerful magnetic fields, driving the cells into harmony and oneness at the morphological level."

"Reprogramming," Klein said, filled with a wonderment that momentarily bypassed his dispassionate cynicism, overwhelmed its chill, subverted it. Perhaps this was the jolt Sybille and Zacharias and Gracchus and the rest felt as they aimed their weapons at animals lost in prehistory but recovered by genetic science, herds trampling the African plains, and falling under deliberate bombardment from the guns of those who shared their condition. More than a jolt, he told himself. A benediction. A joining. Again, that tincture of the numinous. What is happening to me, he asked himself, and felt a pulse of shame.

"Not quite. Reactivating old programs, in a cascade of recapitulation. Your former wife's spine is knitting up, her bones coming together, disrupted muscles and dermis finding their proper locations. The respirocytes gather in her lungs, haematocytes in her corrected vasculature. We should leave now, the process is well begun but will take hours to complete."

"It took weeks for me," Klein said. Not including the drying off, with its stumbling acquisition of a new, fast speech pattern, spookily growing familiarity with alien social ways. The moth crawling damp and twisted from its rejected pupa, cocoon split open to the air, spreading its folded wings. *Faux pas* upon blunder—yet really, all things considered, attaining social mastery with minimal disruption of the deads one moved among, with their waxen skin, now one's own, and their numb thousand-yard stare.

"Rekindling after first death, which you have passed through, is a complex procedure. Much of the postmortem body and its metabolism must be reinvented, so to speak, and reconstructed. Repair of a dead is far simpler, and drying off is greatly accelerated."

Doors slid shut behind them, sealed. A positive pressure airlock. More doors. They stripped off their polymer skins, changed back out of scrubs. Klein donned his linen shirt, patterned cravat, seersucker suit, slipped on his self-sealing boots. The Guidefather dressed again in a bold crimson business suit. Like worshipers in a mystery cult, Klein could not help thinking, returning to the desacralized outer world. He frowned. Enough!

"I hope you will tell me now why I have been brought here half-way across the continent to witness this procedure. Sybille Klein is no longer my wife; I have no special interest in her situation."

"We shall speak further about this in my office. Come."

An elevator took them up smoothly two floors from the medical basement to the administrative center. The ubiquitous cinderblock and undecorated corridors. A functional dark gray carpet muted their footsteps. Deads passed, nodding to the Guidefather, ignoring Klein. Hakim's office was nothing like Chair Bik Liu's at UCLA: it was starkly utilitarian, windowless, with sturdy, cushioned bentwood chairs around a steel-topped desk with embedded equipment. The only break in this Spartan room was a wall-sized display, currently set to deepest tan flecked with craters. After an instant, Klein knew it: human skin. Not quite the African purple-black of his host.

He sat across the table from Hakim, who muttered some command syllables to activate the display. Images began to flash, pause, animate, graph, chart. Klein listened in a dazed state of concentration to the rush of specialist jargon. Antagonistic pleiotropy. NOTCH gene signaling. Secretory pathway organelles in vast, catalogued order. Synthetic telomeres and centromeres to help lengthen lifespan indefinitely. Code adopted from the extremophile bacterium *Deinococcus radiodurans*, with its fancy redundant genome and resistance to radiation damage, and clues to emulating this process with devices at the molecular scale. The proliferative potential of stem and progenitor cells restored and amplified. None of it made absolute sense, even under Hakim's stately tuition, but the words and images flew by, slowly accreted in his mind.

"Yes, yes, Guidefather," he said finally. "Enough, please. You know my studies are in the humanities, not the sciences. But it seems to me that none of this explains a damned thing. Who developed these techniques? None of the warms seem to know, for all their media gossiping and academic conferences, and nobody here in the Cold Towns is telling. I smell a rat, Dr. Hakim, but for the life of me"—he gave a brief hard smile—"I still can't conceive the motives of those who invented these miracles, and cool fusion, and a dozen other innovations, and then just—" He broke off, bit his lip. "Nor what you and Imam Sabbāh expect of me. And perhaps of my ex-wife." He sat back, irritable and frustrated.

Hakim regarded him, imperturbable. He deactivated the display. "I believe Guidefather Sabbāh has inducted you as an Adjutant in the Conclave of the Rekindled. Of the Deads."

"Yes, Whatever that means. Also an Acolyte, which has a disturbingly religiose ring to it. What are we deads now, the seeds of a cult? Or an army?"

"Neither." Hakim gave him a dazzling smile, then, and rose. "A fusion of mysticism and science, perhaps. An unexpected emergent from our condition, and its source. More of that later."

Klein stood up. "You haven't told me what you want of me. I have no taste for hunting quaggas and dodos and Tyrannosaurus rex in the game parks of Africa, like some. Like Sybille, in fact. I've paid my corporate dues, my insurance investment covered all the costs of my rekindling, what else the hell—"

"Why, Jorge," Jamal Hakim told him, "we expect great things of you." He took his arm, and led him out of the room. "Certainly, let us stay with the religious terminology you introduced. Yes. Dr. Klein, you are chosen. Consider yourself in the role of a reborn Paul of Tarsus. You have been selected to be our Apostle to the Warms."

Gog Poll: *Are You Man Enough to be a Dead?*

Ya, zinger, zip open your pad and drop some X's in the Spots X Marks.

Gog how it is this year—can't nab a nap of wink for the howling dead things creeping about in the dark.

But can't be bad totally. All that gold, right? And hey, they have a poison stare like you wouldn't believe.

So—you have the stuff to be a dead? Answer our blood-drenched quizette and check out your score. And if you crave those dead pale or dark thighs—maybe you can be dead, too, and *really* score, gross time.

A: **Are your favorite deads**
- ☐ cold-blood vamps with giant prongs?
- ☐ slavering zoms that wanna fuck your brain?
- ☐ rotten corpses in the stench of the grave rave?
- ☐ Archibald Henrietta Stone, the first dick-swap deader?

B: **Why did the dead chicken cross the road?**
- ☐ To get to the Other Side?
- ☐ So its eggs got sucked by Granny?
- ☐ For the Sand Witches there?
- ☐ For the road kill chicks?

C: **When did the first dead like come back?**
- ☐ In 1348, during the Black Death
- ☐ In 1900, when Typhoon Mary was the cook
- ☐ In 2021, when Archibald Henrietta Stone like came back
- ☐ In 29 AD, when Jeezuz jumped off his cross

D: **Are the Cold Towns**
- ☐ really cold party scenes?
- ☐ dens of iniquity that should be torched?
- ☐ prisons for the insane?
- ☐ dens of monsters that should be blown to shit?

Inviting Klein the rekindled into his house with languid gestures that surely failed to disguise his anxiety, Framji Jijibhoi smiled in welcome as his wife Ushtavaity stood demurely in pale rose sari and white kerchief, silent, watchful. His hand did not extend to clasp the dead man's. Somehow he could not bring himself to touch that pallid skin. Superstition thrummed in him, as always when he stood too near the object of his scholarly investigations, armored in sociological constructs made by default almost entirely at second hand. He knew how he must appear to his former colleague: Yes, he thought, I am a tall nosy intruder from the exoteric world, the neat Zoroastrian sociologist from a teemingly alien city, once Mumbai, again now Bombay under the picturesque resurgent Raj, more than half a world distant—in its ancient blend of living, dying, dead, imaginary reincarnated—from the Cold Towns and their palpably reborn.

"I'm sorry I'm late," Klein said. "The airline schedules these days…" The dead gave an apologetic shrug. Half a head shorter than his host, he had somehow acquired a force, a kind of *mana*, that Jijibhoi found exquisitely disturbing.

"No, no, come in, come in, Jorge." Beyond the stilted entry deck, the galaxy of Los Angeles stretched its massed blaze against the darkness. "How kind of you to visit. I must confess that until your call I had not expected the pleasure of your company following your… transition." He added hastily, babbling, "Despite the recent rise in tourism, deads are sighted so rarely outside your gated domains, you know. The tables are turned; my secondhand knowledge bows to your immersion at the life-death interface. But oh dear—" and he forced himself after all to take the dead's hand, "we were so sorry to hear of the attack on Zion and the death, the, the second death of Sybille."

"She is recovering, Framji. Her injuries were severe, but not beyond the healing powers of rekindling. But thank you for your concern. Madam Jijibhoi, how good to see you again, and how generous of you to invite me. Here, I brought a little Chassagne-Montrachet from the Cold Town cellars."

"You are welcome, welcome, sir," she murmured, bowing, "Thank you, we do enjoy a nice Chardonnay," and immediately departed for the kitchen with the cooler-wrapped bottle.

"I have a hundred questions, dear friend. I hope you will not object too much if I seek to remedy my ignorance? But come, sit down at the table, my wife has prepared something for our supper, I hope you still share our fondness for baby goat marinated in red chillies?"

"I look forward to it. I have to confess, though, that my taste buds have not survived the transition in great abundance. It is as you predicted. We eat and drink mainly for nutrition. But your wife's chillies—yes, I'm certain they will brighten my mouth."

Ushta came to the dining room with the Chardonnay in an ice bucket, another bottle, opened, breathing, of Cabernet Sauvignon which Jijibhoi poured, then swiftly returned with bowls of dhan daar patio, rich with the odor of turmeric, dhan saak, its basmati rice thickened with vegetable daal, eggs on potatoes and spinach. Wine flowed. They ate, Klein with every appearance of appreciation, and Jijibhoi spoke of university politics, hilarious scandals of the sociology department, Klein's reassignment as professor mortuus. They finished with ranginak, its wheaten biscuit flavored with dates, walnuts, ground pistachio, cardamom, cinnamon, washed down with hot, dark tea. The specter of this happy repast stripped of its tastes, its odors, its evoked memories filled the Parsee with horror and a renewed determination to avoid rekindling at all costs. Far better to lie at last in the walled Tower of Silence, parching in the hot sun, gnawed to the bone by vultures, than to abandon all the joys of the flesh and live forever in the half-life seated across the table from him.

"Let's clean up this midden and move into the living room. We've still got lots to talk about." They each carried plates and bowls and cutlery to the kitchen, although it fell to Ushtavaity to rinse and sort into the cleaner. Jijibhoi found snifters and a darkly luminous cut crystal decanter. He lowered the living room lamps so the galaxy of street lights and the true sky were visible through the windows, activated a hushed performance of the madrigals the deads favored. He poured brandy, Klein sipped, set the glass aside, waited patiently with that long and meaningless stare.

"I hope you don't mind if I'm frightfully direct, Jorge."

"You're dying to have me dish the dirt," Klein said. "So to speak. It's fine, speak freely. We are old friends."

"All right." He found himself fidgeting; Ushta came in and settled herself gracefully in an armchair. "Last time we met, Jorge, you were frantic. Obsessed. In despair. You vanished to Africa—"

"Zanzibar."

"Yes, yes. And died as mysteriously as Sybille, the first time she passed. And now, not all that much later, here you are. Serene, or at least relaxed. Not the bundle of jumpy nerves I recall."

"Framji," his wife said, in a warning tone.

"It's fine, Madam Jijibhoi," the dead man said. "Framji and I have already agreed—"

"Ushtavaity," she said. "Ushta."

"I'm sorry?"

"My name. Do you know, it's extraordinary, we have never formally exchanged names. Please call me Ushta."

"Why, thank you, Ushta." The bleak coolness in the man's voice is an artifact of his condition, Jijibhoi told himself. He does not mean insult. Or does he? That desperate fool Dolorosa showed more passion than this, but of course he was an outcast from the Cold Towns. Who could say what such isolation might do to a man dead once to the living and rejected again by the dead?

"You know that my central interest is the social structure of rekindled society," Jijibhoi said. "Less so the nuts and bolts. But really, it's becoming clear that the mysteries quite literally embodied in the deads are the key to this emerging, parallel civilization in our midst. Yet we are denied knowledge of these mysteries and the technique by which dead warms are transformed into, well, living deads. I mean, the simplest things. Do you really age slowly, or not at all? The rumor accepted by the intelligentsia is that of course you are just slowed, aging retarded by a factor of 10 or 20, even as the crackpots of church, mosque, and gog shriek that you are deathless zombies and vampires. Obviously it's too early to decide the matter by simple inspection. Yes, we'll have our answer in a century or a millennium. But it would be much more obliging if you could just, you know, *tell us.*"

Coolly, Klein said, "In the last seven years, fifteen rekindled have been kidnapped and vivisected, according to our information."

"These were the acts of unhinged rogues and terrorists," Ushtavaity said, wringing her hands. "They were butchered on camera. We've all watched the stereos."

"Eleven were butchered on camera. The other four were abducted and taken, according to our information, to black ops labs here and in Qatar. The governments involved are now familiar with the results of our advanced medical technology. They are certainly attempting to reverse-engineer it." Klein sighed. "It won't do them any good, of course."

Jijibhoi doubted that or perhaps, he thought, he was stung by Klein's arrogance. "Come now. They have access to the finest minds in the world. Neuroscientists, genomicists, specialists in epigenetics and the thermodynamics of nanotech. It can't be that difficult. You are... living proof...of the technology."

"True in principle. But it would take hundreds of years to digest what they've peeled out of our comrades."

"But this is just assertion. Whistling, if you'll forgive the expression, past the graveyard. Moore's law, Jorge. Yes, it's slowed to a snail's pace, but the power of technology does still double and redouble. What could possibly prevent us from learning—"

"You don't even know where the information came from, or who developed it. And it's been fifteen years now."

Jijibhoi felt his shoulders slump. Stalemate. It really was like quizzing a cultist. A wave of sadness moved through him.

"The Venter labs, presumably. Gates and Allen funding. NSA connectome cryptographers. Something like that. What matters is—"

"What matters, dear Framji," Klein said with glacial certainty, "is the source of the information, not its implementation."

Abruptly, the sour mood of exhaustion was dispelled. Fire rushed through his limbs. Jijibhoi leaned forward, and from the corner of his eye saw that his wife was also intent. "What source? What are you talking about?"

"I could require you both to sign a non-disclosure agreement with hefty penalties, but what I'm about to disclose would make such penalties chickenfeed. So I'll simply trust you both," Klein said. "They decrypted a message signal from space." His dead eyes glittered. "From deep space." He watched them closely, as if judging and recording their reactions. "From a star in the Andromeda galaxy."

Five

"The only obsession everyone wants: 'love.' People think that in falling in love they make themselves whole? The Platonic union of souls? I think otherwise. I think you're whole before you begin. And the love fractures you. You're whole, and then you're cracked open."

Philip Roth, *The Dying Animal*

Hester Solomon and her husband Moshe collected Klein at Heathrow and they took an autonomic limo into London. Moshe was a British investment banker, specializing in South American stochastic arbitrage. His doctorate was in a field of mathematics so rarefied Klein could not even begin to understand its uses or principles. Hester, of course, was a good upper middle class Jewish wife and mother, as striking as her mother had been as a young woman. Sybille had introduced her to Moshe Solomon.

"Marjorie Morningstar," Klein said, with a smile. They had both loved the literature of the mid-20th century as children: Wouk, Chaim Potok, Malamud, Roth. He waited until she stepped forward for a hug and quick kiss on the cheek.

"Asher Lev," she retorted. Said warmly, he could not help thinking. Warm, a warm, a female warm. Far, a long long way to go. But that was *Sound of Music*, a different tale of love and persecution entirely.

"No artist I," he demurred, as tradition required. "An apostate, that I'll confess."

In the spacious back of the limo, the eldest son, Eliezer, sat shyly beside his uncle Jorge and said almost nothing, in a refined transatlantic accent. The boy was in Harrow uniform, sans top hat and cane:

pale gray trousers, white shirt with black silk tie, and dark blue jacket. In his lap was what Klein surmised was the classic straw boater. The very model of an upper-middle-class English schoolboy. If he was freaked out by the proximity of a dead, he did not allow his discomfort to show.

The adults exchanged mandatory words of sympathy, explanation and conjecture concerning Sybille's state and its cause—had the fire-bombing been a venomous sectarian attack? A work of political terrorism? The expression of some internal factional dispute among the deads themselves? Klein quickly put an end to that. Police forces and security were looking diligently into the atrocity, but no, emphatically there was no slightest reason to suspect fractures within the closed world of the rekindled. This was no more than a slanderous attempt by media jackals to blacken the victims. "Like Hitler and the Reichstag," suggested Eli, and an uncomfortable silence fell. Hester said, quickly, "Mom and dad are waiting for us at the hotel, Jorge. They flew in yesterday. It's quite the meeting of the clans."

Klein groaned. "So much for leaving the dead to bury the dead, as the Christians so prophetically put it. The parents declined to convey their bereavement when I called them with news of Sybille's second death. That *shiksa*. Father all but hung up in my ear."

"Well. *Shiva* was sat. You're not only dead, Jorge, you're *dead*. I'm sorry, it's awful."

"And yet they're here, you say."

Moshe told him in his rumbling voice, "They have seen you on TV, read your interviews. You have become a notable part of the cultural landscape, you know."

"And they want to shut me up."

Hester glanced at the 12-year-old. "This should wait."

"Don't mind me," Eli said with a crafty grin. "The other chaps and I can't see what all the fuss is about, really. Well, Luton had a few snarky things to say but I soon set him straight." He rubbed the knuckles of his right fist on his trousered knee, and gave his uncle a bland look. Klein laughed softly.

"Good for you, kid. We deads need a few more people like you in our corner."

The driverless car dropped them at the Montagu Place Hotel, where a slender Pakistani porter took his minimal luggage.

"Not five star, Jorge," Moshe said apologetically, "but those are getting rather stuffy about…"

"Dead Jews."

"Not quite. Live Jews have no trouble getting a suite at Claridge's or the Langham. It's an old-fashioned city in many respects. The traditional bigotries pass eventually, making way for the new."

Moshe checked them in and took the boy up to the Solomons' small suite. Hester led Klein into a snug bar where his parents sat drinking vodka and trying not to look uncomfortable. Sybille's parents sat across from them, utterly at ease. British consular diplomats interfaced with the Foreign Service of the Department of State, George and Anna Palmer were currently binational attaches at Brussels. He had not seen them during their quick visit to Zion Cold Town following their daughter's medical crisis, but he had exchanged brief messages, explaining that Sybille would probably recover completely from her brutal ordeal. Now he shook their hands as everyone rose, hugged his mother, bowed to the cold countenance of his unyielding father.

"I'm glad to find you well, sir."

"Since you're here, you might as well find a seat." It was closest the old man could come to a concession.

"Thank you. Mother, you look lovely."

"My handsome son!"

Formulae, unreeling the clichés. Clowns, it was true, they were all clowns. Endless emptiness. Sundered. Yet the pain was gone, he realized. If there was no joy in this reunion, neither was there grief nor anger nor the old demand for acknowledgment. Alive, he had been broken until Sybille healed him, or rather he and Sybille colluded in a mutual embrace that excluded the sting of such rejection. She died, impossibly she died; he was not merely broken again but desolate, driven by a need that choked his heart and made him a mad thing, obsessed and futile. And now, he saw finally, all that anguish was drained away. He felt nothing for these people, no love, no yearning for acceptance, even as he felt no animosity nor resentment. He was free.

And it meant nothing at all.

"Can I get anyone another drink," Klein said.

In an atmosphere at once chilly and desperately contained, Moshe called them a limo and instructed it to bear all eight of them the 16 kilometers to Gants Hill. "Not Orthodox, Reformed—but they keep kosher," he promised. There was a palpable breach in the lowering mood when the name of the restaurant-pub was revealed, antique gold against smoky oak: *Bangers & Mashugana*. Eli laughed out loud. "Bangers and mash! What an outrage!"

"I don't even know what that is," Klein told the boy. "Not kippers steeped in their own haggis, I hope."

The boy laughed harder, tears running down his face. The strain had wound the child up more than any of the adults had cared to notice. "It's just sausages and whipped potato, with lashings of gravy and tomato sauce. Like, ketchup. Yummy!"

Dubious, the Klein parents followed their daughter's husband into a low-ceilinged, noisy, smoky cavern. A great bar-counter made a polished horseshoe in the center of the beamed room, and men and women shamelessly drank together, laughing, nudging each other, calling their orders. It might have been a stage set. Perhaps it was, a calculated tourist trap. In one corner a pair of Jews with payot curling down before their ears, and dark felt hats, played chess, ignoring the innocent vice on every hand. Small tables were scattered along one wall. Three of these awaited their party, squeezed together, cutlery and linen already in place.

"They know you here?" Klein asked.

"They know me everywhere, dear chap. Come come, take our seats, the girl will be along in a moment for our orders so make up your minds quick-smart, they don't mess about in this pub." Moshe gestured; a waiter brought them beer, stout, wine in a tall flagon, a soda for the boy.

"You're quite certain this is kosher?" Mrs. Klein said, quite certain that it couldn't possibly be.

"Absolutely. We're in the middle of London's Jewish district. Forget Golders Green. I'll have Yorkshire pudding," he told the plain middle-aged woman in an apron that reached to her knees. "Jorge, I

122

recommend the steak and kidney pie with vegetables. As for you antique folks, you might care for something you recognize—a rare steak with a baked potato, some grilled bream, order anything but pizza or burgers, they'd throw us to the wolves."

Voices rose, plates were piled high and then a moment later, it seemed, miraculously emptied. Desserts made the same magical transition from being to nothingness. No words of substance were exchanged. Klein stolidly munched his untasting way through the provender, pretending enjoyment. He was not unhappy, nor was he happy. He thought of Arthur Schopenhauer: "The two enemies of human happiness are pain and boredom." Here and now he felt no pain, and not really boredom either, but the absence of those two enemies did not clear any space for happiness. He shoveled up his sweet, washed it down with a half and half, a mix of mild ale and bitter. Inside his altered body, nanocytes tore the molecules apart, sorted them, broke down the alcohol before it could reach his brain. Could it be, he thought, that I am at least…content? It seemed impossible. Well. He prepared to tell these people, his relatives and former in-laws, some truths of that altered condition, and what it meant to be a dead on the hoof, no longer living but assuredly still kicking. I am the Apostle, he thought, to the Gentiles. To the Genitaled. To the Gendered. I am the dickless, ball-less wonder come to bear improbable testimony to the very humans least likely to pay me any attention. Except the kid, he thought. Except the boy, Eliezer.

For the first time in his life, he felt the poignant stab of a wish for a child of his own.

BBC Gogcast transcript
1 October 2037

Our Science & Society mavenette, Dr. Jane Makwe, speaks with Professor Jorge Klein, spokesperson for the Conclave of the Rekindled, and himself a dead for four years. Jane spoke with Jorge from her den in Edinburgh.

JANE: Welcome to the rant, Jorge. You don't mind a bit of informality?

JORGE: It might be more professional, Dr. Makwe, if you addressed me as Professor Klein.

JANE: Oooh, stuffy! Let's keep it friendly and light, shall we, Jorge? I mean, we're dishing some pretty gruesome shit here.

JORGE: As you wish.

JANE: Jorge hails from Argentina, clubbies, and you'd think looking at the way his name's spelled he'd go by "Georgie." Nup, "Whore-hey" it is.

JORGE: I was born in Buenos Aires, Jane, but we moved to California when I was four. I hold joint citizenship.

JANE: Cool—a citizen of the world! Highly fash! But hey, don't you like lose your citizenship when you like die?

JORGE: No. My passport is still active. But it's certainly a question currently under review in both our countries.

JANE: But us Brits don't have any deads. It's a Yank thing. Why's that? Isn't it like restraint of trade or something? Not to mention human rights.

JORGE: I understand your concern, Jane, but the rekindling process was developed by Americans in the United States, and the process is proprietary.

JANE: Protected by megacorp patents, you mean?

JORGE: Actually, no. The matter is vexed. The Conclave have their hands tied at the moment because the Supreme Count of the United States has declared all the relevant techniques to be a munitions issue, and anyone selling or transporting that information to other nations would be subject to trial for treason and the most extreme penalties.

JANE: They get offed?

JORGE: At the very least.

JANE: Ha ha. I like that. You mean they'd be executed with no chance of getting reborn as a dead.

JORGE: Precisely.

JANE: Grim. Ironic, then, that Jules Lagrange, notorious secret-blower from the early years of the mill, is now a dead hiding in San Diego Cold Town.

JORGE: That's the kind of nonsense retailed on the crackpot gogs. Mr. Lagrange is not an American citizen. He was born in Belgium and so is not eligible for rekindling. As far as I know, he remains in custody in Guantanamo.

JANE: Maybe they don't tell you everything, Jorge.

JORGE: Do they tell *you* everything, Jane? By the way, what kind of doctorate do you hold?

JANE: Snippy now! Well, I'll tell you, it's not like I'm hiding some dirty secret that would excite Jules and his gang. I'm a haematologist, with a degree from St. Andrews and postdoc studies at Baylor. For the sports fans watching, a haematologist is an expert in blood. Which handily leads me to my next question: what can you tell us about heterochronic parabiosis?

JORGE: I'm sorry, what?

JANE: When the blood vessels of old and young mice were spliced together in experiments back in the oughts, the old guys got young and the young mice got older.

JORGE: I suppose that's possible. But it has nothing—

JANE: Let's get technical, doc. Heterochronic parabiosis increases hepatocyte proliferation and renews the cEBP-alpha complex, giving the old buggers a kick-start of youthful vigor. Blood, man, fresh young blood. Isn't that what spices up the deads?

JORGE (laughs): Really, you're not serious. Deads as *vampires*? Blood suckers? Dr. Makwe, that's the coarsest slur seen on the most rabid gogs. Have you ever heard the term *blood libel*? The Nazis accused the Jews—

JANE: Oooh, touched a nerve, have we?

"That went well," Jamal Hakim said in his ear.

125

The stupidity of it all. Klein said, "Look, Dr. Hakim, I'm by nature a solitary, introverted man, always have been. Death had not made me magically more congenial. I'm just not cut out for this kind of advocacy. You want me to soothe the warms down, and I'm just inflaming them." He paused. "Unless that's your intention. Am I a Judas goat?"

"Truly, Jorge, that interview was a success. You showed again that we are not chilly monsters to be feared, that we are offended by slurs and attacks. The warms watching that gog will feel a deeper empathy for us than they would have if you'd brushed aside that woman's offensive questions with a smile and a quip. That would be the response of a practiced politician, which is to say a corporate crook and conniver. You are not a Judas goat, Professor. You are not leading warms into a trap. Quite the reverse. We are their future and their salvation, however much they fear us. This is part of your training, Jorge. I meant it when I said you are to be our Apostle to the Gentiles."

"None of the Apostles came to an especially enviable end."

"We need not be overly literal in our figures of speech. But look here, you mention your tendency toward solitary introversion. When you return to the Cold Towns, we will do something about that."

"What now? Not just Guidefather, but Panderer-in-Chief?" No response, defense, angry retort in his ear. "Listen, I was scarcely a virgin when Sybille and I married, you know. Christ, I was nearly thirty. And we had our fun with others during the marriage. I've known the bodies and minds, if not the love, of fair women and dark, more than a few of them. I don't need your damned help."

"That's not what I meant, and you know it. Still, I remind you that since your drying off, you've conspicuously sulked in your tent. Not least during your travels."

Klein thought suddenly of the wandering gang into which Sybille had fallen so swiftly, roaming the world as tourists of the expired. Had she been inserted into that aimless set by psychologists, Conclave specialists enacting the role of marriage brokers, some *shadchan* arranging plural *shidduchim* for the newly dead? The prospect promised some entertainment value, but really it revolted his deepest essence. He and Sybille, the one lasting liaison of his life, had been an accident abetted by their simultaneous presence in the Hanging Gardens, favorite refectory of the university scholars. Like and unlike,

Jew and Gentile, teacher and student, congruent in the shared culture of centuries, different enough not to stale, sufficiently akin to merge flesh and mind and soul into a dyadic unity greater than he had ever supposed feasible for a man isolated by intellect and temperament. But that was the old Jorge, he told himself. That was the Klein before death had sucked him dry, drained away the warm juices from their conjoined link. Parabiosis indeed, he thought. And now their blood was a construct of old fluids and prowling haematocytes, oxygen borne through the raceways of their blood vessels inside carbon and silicon cages stronger and more commodious and longer lived than anything devised by bumbling evolution. Maybe the brokers of the postmortal cult he had been snatched into might bond him anew with comrades whose company he could enjoy, women he might lie beside in the remote yet oddly tender embraces of the dead.

"All right," he said, in the swift code that had been impressed upon his brain by machines grown out of algorithms from a star in an entirely different galaxy, "all right, set me up."

"You don't *look* very dead, you deads," the interviewer said. "In fact, you seem rather quick on your feet."

"Calling us *deads* is a vulgarism, you know. The preferred term is 'rekindled.'"

"Yet you do use it yourselves."

"Well, it's a traditional defensive move by persecuted groups to borrow terms of abuse. Gays called themselves *queer*. Black singers took up the gangster use of *nigga*. But I'm also of Jewish stock. Would you sit there with a smile and call me a kike?"

"Didn't mean to tread on your toes, love." Brine Di Stefano was an epicene specimen, languid in Klein's borrowed Bunche Hall professorial office. Sunlight streamed through his bouffant hair, each strand crisp and surrounded by a glow. "But now I'm going to have to. *The New York Times* is the gog *de référence*, you know, so we have to get the record straight. So to speak." He smirked. "It's often said that the drive behind rekindling is an evasion of reality, a flight from life. Some say you willfully block your transition to the afterlife. Even the Mormon Atheists find evidence in their scriptures that you are the new Nephilim, to be abjured and cast out."

Klein smiled. "I'm not tall, as you see. I believe the imaginary Nephilim were Giants in the earth."

"We speak here in symbols, professor. Let's not nitpick. I can be specific. A senior member of the White House staff, speaking off the record—"

"If she spoke off the record, why are you quoting her?"

Di Stefano brushed this aside. "This person whose gender must remain undisclosed said that the Conclave of the Dead has criminally evaded payment of taxes for more than a decade, is using highly classified information stolen from Federal assets, and plans the corruption of the American people. Comment?"

"I'm not a lawyer, Brine, nor am I a tax expert. Still, as I understand it, taxes have never been levied on the deceased since the founding of this Republic, unless you count the estate tax. I grant you that the President's party is often accused of gaining office through the franchise of the dead—and I don't mean people like me, who are currently entirely *dis*enfranchised. Does this seem just to you and your readers?"

"Okay, sweetie, I'm with you. Let me track back a step. Revival from death is a kind of ultimate eugenics. Isn't death designed as the proper termination of life, without which living has no meaning?"

Klein had heard all this a hundred times by now, and his mind was stocked with a hundred glib one-liner ripostes. He put them aside, leaned forward, spoke carefully. This intellectual buffoon represented a serious newsgog; surely some of its readers were capable of thinking beyond clichés.

"Eugenics is a tainted word. Why? Only because of the way it was abused a century ago in the era of fascism, Nazism, and Soviet and Chinese communism. Not to mention in this country, when people of limited intelligence were forcibly castrated for the alleged good of the race."

"By 'race' you mean—"

"You know perfectly well what I mean. The distinction needs to be drawn between that kind of atrocity and the free choices individuals make for themselves and their children."

"Oh, so it's just fine for some bigoted redneck or Chinese commissar to—"

"If they're making free choices not imposed by the state or corporations or faiths or any other kind of forcible—"

A wave of the hand. "Rekindling is an affront to the Lord, according to Cardinal von Sachsen. It is a regressive infantile evasion of maturity, says the New York Directorate of Psychoanalysis. I could spiel out the quotes, but you're surely aware of these arguments. How do you answer them? I have to tell you, I find them persuasive."

Klein sat back, sighed. "You've heard of the Stockholm Syndrome?"

"I believe so. I took a course in Asymmetrical Warfare at Princeton, actually." The interviewer frowned. "You mean the way a captive or victim of torture paradoxically bonds to her oppressor. That's a facile analogy."

Klein was remorseless. "If a child is threatened with death by a congenital heart defect, should that go untreated?"

"Plainly, not. A repair of localized—"

"A soldier is shot in the field of battle and bleeds out. His biometrics report an EEG crisis. In moments he will be dead. Should the medics zip him up in a body bag, untreated?"

"Certainly not. This is sophistry! We were talking about people already dead who are subject to a grossly unnatural procedure that some ethicists claim produces a 'zombification' of its victims."

Klein bared his teeth, then smiled. "Do you fear I might lunge and eat your brain?"

"Stranger things have happened." Di Stefano returned a dazzling grin. "Don't bite the messenger, doc."

"Messengers can catch Stockholm Syndrome too. Open your eyes and look at the evidence, Brine. Death has always been an abomination, a horrible accident of evolution. Nobody designed death. It's an evolutionary kludge. We're disposable. Our genes don't care about our survival once we've multiplied them through reproduction. But now we have scientific means to reverse that blunder. Rekindling is no more unethical nor Satanic than having damaged teeth replaced by genomic implants, or fixing your worn-out knee cartilage or heart with autologous stem cells reprocessed from your own skin."

"So saith the Chamber of Commerce of the Cold Towns. Philosophers and ordinary folks vehemently disagree. You've crossed a line.

Some are anticipating a severe government crackdown. What will be the response of the Conclave if and when that comes?"

Klein stood up. "It's been delightful chatting with you, sir. Please don't forget to mention the Stockholm Syndrome argument in your piece. If you need a quote to support that, look at Keats."

"The poet?" Brine Di Stefano nodded. "Ah. 'Half in love with easeful Death.'"

"'Call'd him soft names in many a mused rhyme.'"

"Point taken." Ushered to the door, shaking Klein's hand, the journalist said with every evidence of sincerity: "I just hope you guys have good guns and lawyers, when *Der Tag* comes."

Albany Cold Town was literally cold on Christmas Eve, 2037. Strictly speaking, it was part of the city of Cohoes rather than the State capital, but the name had stuck. Jorge Klein took an autonomic cab north from Albany along 787 beside the Hudson. Icicles glittered in bare branches in the streets below, and a little fall of snow sifted down. The Conclave had taken over the Van Schaick Island Country Club, purchasing it outright for a fabulous sum to the fury of its dispossessed members but with the connivance of three members of its Board of Directors including the President and Treasurer, each signed up for rekindling. Its lush championship golf course was now a grid of graceless cinderblock structures, heavily walled, newly braced against attack from the lawless and the law alike. Klein entered the redoubt, displaying proof of his bona fides.

"Come in, come in." The house of strangers was like any other, but he was expected, a notable guest; clearly word had gone ahead from Jamal Hakim. He was to be integrated more fully into the community of the deads, the better to perform his duties for the Conclave. "Welcome, welcome, welcome." Gently they touched and nudged him; after all this time, their waxy skin and staring gaze no longer dismayed him. He was one of them, he knew their thousand-yard stare from within, it was his own condition. "Hello," he said, "hello, hello."

A trio circled about him as he met the residents, two handsome women and a ratty-looking man with a distant but somehow droll demeanor. It was unsaid but immediately understood: these were to be his companions, his set, his crew. They made themselves known to him as the occasion arose, unobtrusively. Here was Francine, slim, elegant, perhaps fifty, a *goyishe* version of his mother, perhaps. And a pretty young third-generation Korean. "Mi-Yun," she said, placing her hand on her breast. "Please don't say 'Me Tarzan,' it gets very, very old." He nodded, amused. And the short fellow with the beaky nose was Tom, an experimental picotechnologist, whatever that was. Finally they bore him away to his guest room, his small suite, in fact, bringing wine and a plate of cookies. "If you decide to make Albany your home base for a while, we'll move you into the main house," Tom told him.

In the night, after all the formalities were completed, he lay beside Francine in the darkness, listening to her breathe. He had decided it would be crass to choose Mi-Yun for this first encounter. Francine was not the first dead woman he had been intimate with, but none of his early experiments had been satisfactory. In the earliest days after his rekindling, he'd been informed again and again by the technicians that he was no longer a sexual being, not in any traditional sense, perhaps in no sense at all. The process altered not the genitalia but the brain, the gusts and flows of hormone secretions, the mechanisms of arousal and performance. He was a eunuch now, as were they all, male and female. The senses remained alert, however, and a numb craving for contact, the bleak reassurances of the grave. He placed his hand on Francine's elbow, where it rested against his ribs, and heard her breathing alter. Slowly he stroked her forearm, clasped her hand lightly. She murmured sleepily; they said nothing in words; they slept.

Christmas morning was chilly, sub-zero, snow crisp on the flattened ground where well-heeled local golfers had once swung their irons in more propitious weather. Klein and Francine met the others for a quick breakfast, dressed warmly, went out under a sky of cloud pregnant with more snow. Church bells rang in the distance, carried with sharp clarity under the clouds. In the traditional houses to the north of the Cold Town, the children of the warms no doubt did all the traditional things that drove their parents nuts: noisily tearing open boxes and plastic cartons, squabbling, shouting happily at

131

the tops of their voices, jumping on parental beds, banging drums, blowing trombones. *Santa's been here, Santa's been here!* None of that for us, Klein thought, and was relieved. He recalled the pledge he and Sybille had made: no children for us, no rug-rats, no heartbreak and responsibility, no hostages to fortune. No joy, either. But now, he told himself, we have our own futures. We are our own futures. We need not fantasize an extended duration through offspring or in a magic afterlife where we wait in bliss to rejoin them; we are our own replacements, dead but deathless. Arrows flung into a future that surely would become ever stranger, decade by decade, in increments perhaps of centuries, millennia, years falling away and drifting like snowflakes…

"We did this when we were kids." Mi-Yun let herself fall back in a mound of snow, ooffed, flung out her leather-jacketed arms and dragged them up and down. "Angel wings!"

"Not in California, land of the sun," Klein said. "And not in Buenos Aires either. It did snow there once, thirty years ago, after I'd left for America with my Mom and Dad. None before that for another ninety years." He found a curious impulse rising in his breast, bent, scooped up two handfuls of granular snow, crushed them into a ball, looked around. Tom stood looking across the Hudson, back to them; Klein flung his snowball, caught the man in the small of his back.

"Hey! No fair!"

Francine joined in, then Mi-Yun, with Tom pelting Klein so hard that his hat flew off. Distanced from himself, Klein marveled. These were deads? These crazy lunatics playing like kids, himself included? Well, why not? If the world was a vortex of meaninglessness, as it was, there was ample space for the *acte gratuit*. If all human activity was the empty capering of clowns in a plastic empty world, let us all be clowns at play, he thought. *C'est moi, Camus*—yes, regard that French existentialist's childhood football fixation, his ferocious smoking, his daredevil and finally self-slaying driving, even though he was not at the wheel of the Facel Vega when he died. Could that intoxication with being and nothingness be the explanation? One worth copying? The deads as rebels, whose cause was to be without a cause. "When he rebels, a man identifies himself with other men and so surpasses himself," Camus had written, "and from this point of view human solidarity is metaphysical."

But the playful impulse drained quickly. He dropped his handful of snow, walked away toward the naked deciduous trees and brush at the water's edge. Shivering, he pulled his coat more tightly about him. His toes felt chilled through boots and heavy socks. Gloved fingers touched his arm. Francine, he thought, and turned, but it was Tom.

"Saw your interview on the *Times* gog. What an idiot. Where do they find these poseurs?"

"Brine was okay," Klein said. "He was treading the party line. It's up to us to change it."

"Or stay out of the line of fire. Not that I'm criticizing you for—"

"Understood. The Conclave Elders anticipate a Reichstag fire followed by a *Kristallnacht*. I'm doing what I can to help avert it, but it's a long trudge up the hill of fear and misunderstanding and guile and simple stupidity."

"Yeah." Tom gestured at the barricaded blockhouse structures of the Cold Town. "We country boys don't know much about those old Krauts, Jorge, but we remember Ruby Ridge and…what was it called? Those crazy cultists the government torched to the ground?"

"David Koresh," Klein said. "The Branch Davidians, in Texas."

"Them too, I guess. No, those others down in Florida. Crazy as loons, but shit. Burned out the whole goddam town. Thousands of people killed, and no rekindling for them."

"Clearwater. Yes. That's what concerns us. That's what I'm trying to head off."

A hand touched his other arm. Francine. Very well. These were to be his closest companions, his pals, his affinity group. He touched her glove, nudged her shoulder.

"We should be getting back."

Snow was falling again, harder now. It squeaked and crackled under their boots.

Half reclining in his medical bed, Mick Dongan was reduced from the boisterous, vulgar monologist Klein remembered. The anthropologist was eaten out from within, it was plain to see, by cancer. In the final stages of cachexia, it seemed from his sunken etched cheeks and the knotted joints of his exposed wrists hanging like the lumps of bone they were from arms piteously atrophied.

"Come in, for Christ's sake, Jorge. I know I look like shit. But at least I'm not dead, like some people." Dongan emitted a ghastly croaking laugh, coughed for half a minute, breath rasping in his caved-in, bony chest. Oxygen went into his lungs from transparent tubes run to his nostrils, but it brought no flush to his face. "It's not catching, dude."

"It's been some time," Klein said, and drew a chair closer to the bed. "You'll have heard about Sybille's little adventure in the bombing at Zion."

"Bloody nasty, that. Pour me some juice, there's a good fellow. Bastards won't let me have anything stronger." He slurped a mouthful of pale lemon liquid through a bent straw, swirled it in his mouth, screwed up his face, spat it out into a kidney-shaped steel basin. "Looks like piss, tastes worse." He sighed, lay back against the shaped pillow of his elaborate bed, closed his eyes.

After a time, Klein concluded that the dying man had fallen asleep, and stood. Dongan opened his eyes and grinned at him, like a man who has won a bet. Several of his teeth were missing. Lost from the shrinkage of the disease? Rotted inside his head? This was no traditional cancer, Klein knew. Bitter rumor-mongers were already blaming the rekindled for its origin and spread. Why would they do that? Pick up new customers, like funeral directors fallen on hard times in a place stricken by good health?

"Siddown, Jorge. I have to get this off my chest."

A wave of weariness flooded through Klein. Last minute repentance, confession of misdeeds, pleas for forgiveness. Or could the man be about to declare a windfall for his old best friend, a bequest, perhaps his townhouse on leafy Abbot Kinney Boulevard in Venice?

"I'm not your father confessor, Mick. Not even the right faith. Not any faith, in fact, as you'll recall."

"It's about Sybille. She and I—"

"Hush." He made a quieting motion with one hand, irritated by this banality. "It was the time. We all slept around. I've known about your affair with my wife for years. We hid nothing from each other. Nothing of that kind, anyway."

"Shit, Jorge, don't make it harder than it already is." Breath catching in his throat, shoulders hunching. Stopped. Restarted with a jolt. A deep breath, then slow, shallow intaking of air. Was this Cheyne-Stokes respiration? If so, the man was surely at the very edge of death.

"Have you made arrangements for rekindling?" Klein said. "I didn't see a van outside."

"Not doing it. Refused. World's got enough damned zoms already. No, sorry, sorry, feeble humor. Made up my mind when Sybille asked for rekindling. Not for me."

"You'd prefer to be ashes? Rot into slime in the ground? Don't be absurd, Mick." He hesitated. "I've never known a man with the appetite for living that you had." And would lose, he acknowledged silently, in this resurrection into bleak forever. He wondered if he would have chosen it himself, had death and rekindling not been forced upon him.

Shameless in the proximity of his own nothingness, Dongan put the same thought into words.

"Doesn't seem to have done you a hell of a lot of good, Jorge. Death warmed up." Something caught again in his throat. His face went into rictus. Klein watched him, said nothing. "Still haven't said it. Professor Klein, old chum, I'm making a clean breast of it. Your wife and I were going to abscond together."

"Don't be ridiculous."

"Yeah, yeah, I know it goes against your fairytale romance. The one-and-onlies, despite the bed hopping. The magic dyad. Two souls as one." More coughing. "Lovely fancy, I know, was same with me and Iris, for about five years. And you were heading toward what…a decade? Things change, pal. Christ, look at you. Walking definition of *mutatis mutandis*. Hang on, that's not what I mean. Whatever. But she'd lost that lovin' feeling. The first fine careless rapture was well and truly over. So we made our plans. Then she fucking got sick and died. Don't that beat all?"

Klein stood up. He felt nothing. Not resentment, not bitterness, not a wish to shout or deny or plead or to beat the man's face in. Without a word, he turned and left the room. A racking laugh followed him, and perhaps feeble words, but he could not make out their meaning.

Six

Later he had seen the things that he could never think of and later still he had seen so much worse....He had seen the world change; not just the events; although he had seen many of them and had watched the people, but he had seen the subtler change and he could remember how the people were at different times.

Ernest Hemingway, "The Snows of Kilimanjaro"

Rain was sleeting down when Klein was driven into Moshi town in Tanzania in June, 2039, his non-autonomic taxi piloted by a wizened black man with gleaming teeth, presumably genomic implants courtesy of the Gates Foundation. The deads had selected this shooting season for its dry but moderately cool weather, halfway between the northern monsoonal downpours of the year's start and the southern monsoon in its latter months. Climate change, that universal chaotic disrupter, ruined the forecasts again. Their plane had staggered through dense clouds that blocked any overhead view of the gigantic, hardened, ash-coated mudpie that was the all-but-extinct stratovolcano. A sky island, geologists dubbed this immense mountain, tallest in all of Africa; it was only 150,000 years (would he and his companions live that long? perhaps!) since it erupted last, spewing from its Kibo cone boiling lava that hardened into immense scarps and valleys.

From his room in the New Livingstone Hotel, he gazed now into the rain and saw nothing but a darker shadow, its peaks some twenty miles distant.

The deluge had abated, then stopped, by the time the party of deads arrived in a hired van: the old crew, Zacharias, inevitably in charge, Gracchus the white hunter in all his antique Hemingway glory, Mortimer, Nerita Tracy in a fetching safari suit. And, as arranged, his former wife Sybille. Seeing her step from the van, still young, still beautiful, fully restored, Klein felt washed with grace. Now she was nothing to him. The last remnants of desolation were fled, or, rather, desiccated and swept away by the winds of time.

In the clearing sky, pterodactyls—or were they pteranodons, with those imposing 20-foot wingspans—flurried like black umbrellas caught in an updraft. At their back, high above rolling remnant clouds, the great mountain jutted toward the vacuum of space. Nineteen thousand feet and more above sea level, three and two-thirds miles, the Kibo peak almost a mile higher than this elevated ground. Reports were accurate. No trace of frozen white about its upper reaches. Famously, the legendary snows or glaciers of Kilimanjaro were gone entirely, melted and evaporated or run off for good. Or at least until the bitterly contested spread of cool fusion generators forced the final replacement of carbon fuels and reversed the ruin that warms were inflicting upon their planet. His planet, too, he grudgingly admitted.

Klein withdrew from his window, lay down on the simple bedding. Time enough to greet the other deads when they were rested after the uncomfortable trip. Did this faint ache indicate that he missed the presence of his new crew? No. Those three had their own concerns and interests. Mi-Yun had laughed in disbelief when he mooted the trip to Africa. So be it. Let this be closure.

Alcohol was not advised at altitude, but he found them in the bar off the lobby drinking whiskey sours. When you are dead you are dead all the way, he hummed to himself, and ordered one to be companionable. They greeted him with a knuckled nudge to the shoulder, a bow, a quick comradely hug from Sybille.

"You have become prominent," she said. "Your face on TV rivals the President's."

"And I'm not even running for reelection."

"Still, you've acquired your own share of abuse," Nerita said. The Brazilian was not as lovely as Sybille: sweeping red hair this year, a pert freckled young-middle-aged face, trim as a gym addict.

Somehow she did not have the look of a hunter, even of dead animals. But then neither, after all, did Sybille.

"Oh yes. Raskolnikov Klein. Dr. Kevorkian Klein." He laughed. "They manage to get everything muddled and reversed. We've died, so we are a cult of murderers rather than saviors. We are no longer fated to perish and rot, and so we are obsessed by death. Then again," he said, with a sardonic pause, "some of us do seem to be."

"You have not been without your own obsessions, Klein," said Laurence Mortimer. If the words were biting, even sinister, his tone was guilefully innocent.

"Now resolved, I'm happy to report." He sent Sybille a bland, assessing look, returned his gaze to Mortimer. "At least some of us are not trapped in repetition and neurotic recurrence."

"What's that? Nietzsche or Freud?" Now Mortimer drew his lips tight. "Both con men, wouldn't you agree, and seriously out of date?"

The alcohol was working on them, fuming in their brains despite the dehydrogenase and catalase mimic 'cytes stripping down the ethyl molecules before they could thoroughly poison their higher capacities. There would be no fisticuffs. The deads, despite their fondness for controlled genocide of the extinct, were a placid lot.

"I can't argue with that. But I do have in mind one suggested change in routine. A small addition, you might say, to the fun of slaughtering quaggas and aurochs and dodos. Of course, I'm looking forward to some shooting. I've even taken lessons."

"A change?" Kent Zacharias glowered at him. "And what would that be? A singsong round the fire with the local chapter of People for the Ethical Treatment of Extinct Animals?"

"A little more arduous than that." Klein put down his empty glass precisely in the center of its mat. "I've engaged a guide and a team of porters. After the sport's done, we'll go up Mt. Kili. Quite the view from the top, I'm told."

He looked around at faces betraying consternation, derision, curiosity.

"Boring," said Zacharias. "Ridiculous," said Gracchus. Nerita Tracy glanced up at that; she had been shredding her mat. "I think it sounds interesting, Anthony. Sybille?"

His ex-wife was tranquil. She met Klein's eyes. "An amusing idea. I wish I'd thought of it myself. Perhaps we'll find Hemingway's leopard."

"Long defrosted," Mortimer said, smiling. "And chewed up by pterodactyls."

The first three days trudging and sometimes clambering up the rocky slopes of the mountain were arduous, exhausting even for the renovated bodies of the deads. Already they were above the cloud line. Fortified by hot chocolate and popcorn, lashings of food prepared by the tireless native porters who carried their supplies, filament tents, fusion heaters, and endless quantities of purified water, they slogged through alpine desert terrain that grew ever more alien. Icy rain blew in their faces; Klein reluctantly pulled on a heated mask. On the fourth day, ambient at freezing point, they moved upward through rock pitted like coral, a lunar landscape without trees, plants or animals. The rock tore at their gloved hands, seized and twisted their walking poles. The air thinned. Rebreathers mounted on their backs fed oxygen to their respirocytes, easing the difficulties that caused one gasping porter, without the benefit of high technology, to collapse. These toughened locals had been known to perish on the trail, shaped though they were by conditioning and perhaps evolved adaptation to the heights. In the main they kept out of sight, forging ahead with the tents and sleeping bags and nourishment. They would line up for their tips only at the end of the climb. Klein watched them when he could. If the law allowed, he reflected, this crew of deads would happily shoot into their dark bodies, hack off a head or two, bear the trophies back down in their packs, with customary displays of boredom, to the lands of human habitation.

The Kibo huts, at 15,600 feet elevation, were plain green boxy structures with steep roofs and no windows, mist gusting about them. Other groups were congregated there, as they had been in the base camps lower down, destroying the isolation of hours of brutal climbing. Late in the day, after a rest that seemed to spread pain throughout his body, Klein readied himself for the final assault. Three quarters of a mile into the raw sky.

"This is completely insane," Sybille said, standing beside him in the afternoon sunshine. "I can't believe I agreed to this."

"I believe because it is absurd," Klein said.

"Tertullian, eh. Do you expect to meet God up there, Jorge?"

"*Tat Tvam Asi,*" he said. "Thou art god."

"'That Art Thou,'" she corrected him, pedantically. Always the scholar. Even when she playfully invented her scholarship to mock him. "No need to invoke Yahweh. Or did you mean me? I thought you were over that."

"I never thought you were a goddess, Sybille," he told her. "I thought you were my wife. My loving wife, as I was your loving husband." He shushed her interruption. "But yes, I am over that. Come along, we have a mountain to climb."

Dinner first. No water to wash with. Klein stank, encased in his protective shell. They would climb the rest of the way as the sun sank, and then forward in darkness, step by painful step up the steep path through desolation. Ah yes, thought Klein. Once again, the Dark Night of the Soul. With a glimpse of heaven at the summit, and a view of hell below, with fumaroles.

Mist. Congealed lava. Dust. Temperature below zero. Altitude sickness had them all bowed and head-whirling. Dark, dark. For six terrible hours they clambered like Sisyphus, their own dead flesh the stone they carried upward. Scree tumbled beneath his boots, throwing him off balance. At any moment, Klein thought, I am going to release my grasp on this burden. I will allow gravity's victory. I will crash backward and down, downward to the earth, mutilated by sharp knives of stone. No, he told himself. No, no. This is your clownish challenge to the clowns who held your wife's affection and loyalty. May it kill them all again, he thought, with unaccustomed venom. The thin air is getting to me. Christ. Onward. Upward.

At five in the morning, they attained Gilman's Peak, the first summit. The sun remained below the edge of the world, but the sky was gray with its masked light. They stood like myths above clouds. Nerita was weeping.

The crater stretched out beneath them, empty of its fabled ice, a vast pocket into the throat of the dormant volcano. Wisps of vile gas rose from its fumaroles. If this is not the dried asshole of hell, he thought, it will serve as its apt figuration.

And the sun rose, red and gold, a glory, dispelling Klein's sour mood. Light flooded across Africa, across the birthplace of his species, of the species from which he was born and died and returned. Yes, he thought: returned, as the sun returns. No natural cycle without its tendentious parable, its encouraging metaphor. He caught himself. Enough. This was the moment. Sybille stood touching Ken Zacharias in the tender, evasive way of the dead. Laurence Mortimer placed an arm across Nerita's shoulders. Alone, Klein squeezed his eyes tight.

And still their journey was not complete. Up the blighted, tilted world they struggled for an hour, two hours, more. And here finally was Uhuru Peak, 19,300 feet above the world, the top of Africa. The sky a hard blue. Porters released a swarm of stereo bugs that spun a sparking jeweled haze, memorializing this moment of achievement. All done. Klein fell from his brief moment of epiphany. All emptiness, like the botched landscape. No meaning beyond necessity. I am a philosophical zombie after all, Klein told himself. Thus I refute…everything.

They trudged down the vast mountainside. Down, down, down, would it never come to an end. But Alice had been dreaming her Wonderland; this was brute reality. They were joined at last, on the open grass, green, green, by the crew of porters, many men and youths, caps and brown faces and wide ingratiating or joyfully grinning faces, clapping, *Jambo, Jambo, Kili-man-jaro*, and the tipping began, dollars swiped into paypads, expressions of disbelief, Is *this* all you're paying me? But they had been warned, it was a routine gambit, one must doubt even the rheumy tears in the eyes of an old porter surely too aged and frail to undertake such hazardous work. Gracchus, surprisingly, weakened and swiped the old fellow's pad once more, dollars flowing down from satellites, devalued currency but worth plenty in this landscape haunted by the creatures of the dead. In the far distance, an elephant trumpeted, and at the edge of the grasses Klein watched a pack of running quaggas, white legged, striped at the front like zebras while the colors had run together murkily in the rear, creatures from before the dawn of history. As are we all, Klein told himself, remembering secret messages from the sky.

They returned mile after humming mile to the hotel in a van driven by their guide. Covered in dust, they stank like what they were: death warmed up. Klein refused a whiskey sour toast and headed to his room. Before he left, though, he thanked each of them, touched them lightly in the way of his kind. To Sybille, embracing her lightly, he said, "Thank you for coming."

She moved to place a soft kiss on his cheek; he stepped aside.

"Goodbye, goodbye, goodbye."

He never saw her again.

His passport was seized as he moved through Customs and Immigration at JFK International Airport.

"Your name?"

"Jorge Amadeus Klein. Professor mortuus in the Department of Hist—"

"This document shows a date of death. Are you a rekindled, sir?"

"Yes." No sense in making a fuss about the inane routines, the pretended niceties of the law.

"Please step to one side, sir." The passport remained in the man's hand.

Klein was led to a formidable apparatus. Two beefy, armed Homeland Security officers in gorgeous braid directed him into its maw.

"I'm sorry, gentlemen, I can't do that. I will certainly submit to a physical examination, if that is requested."

"You refuse to obey a lawful and proper instruction given you by duly authorized officials?"

"Not at all. But you must know that a gamma scan, however brief, will risk doing irreparable damage to the very delicate medical equipment inside my body. I'm just asking for the same consideration you routinely extend to travelers with pacemakers or brain implants."

They stared at him with a peculiar intense detestation, but allowed him to pass into an ancillary screened compartment, where he was searched in every crevice, roughly. I'd be passing blood for a week, he thought, if I still had that sort of blood.

142

No further obstacles were placed in his path, but the contents of his luggage, when he checked them in the large odorous men's room, were more jumbled than usual. There'd been nothing illegal or incriminating there, of course, not even the well-wrapped head of a dodo or a monkey's paw. This is intimidation, he realized, pure and simple.

So it had started. Started in earnest, he thought with a spurt of fear, and they will probably haul me away in the middle of the night and lock me up in a dark, foul place. His renovated flesh grew clammy. Pushing through the crowd toward a cab rank, solitary dead in a sea of the quick, he knew that he was scared, really frightened, for the first time in his life. His reborn life. *Nada y pues nada nada nada y pues nada.*

Seven

History can predict nothing except that great changes in human relationships will never come about in the form in which they have been anticipated.

Johan Huizinga, *In the Shadow of Tomorrow*

Three large men in dark business suits stood outside his door in the history department. Clearly they had been tracking his movements, waiting until he returned to the West coast and, more recently, left the protective confines of the Cold Towns.

"Office of Mortuary Affairs," the foremost of the hard-faced Federal officers said, and showed ID that could have been for the city dogcatcher. Klein did not doubt the man's credentials for a moment. The other two loomed behind him, ready to intercept and immobilize Klein if he made a reckless dash for the elevator. "I'm Mr. Jacoby, sir. You will come with us. If you require the services of an attorney, you will have the opportunity to call one when you are in our custody."

Everything in his heritage rebelled against acquiescence in this warrantless arrest. He would be disappeared, like the tens of thousands in Argentina. Or flung into a concentration camp or some stinking Gulag like his ancestral Jews. But no, he told himself, struggling to retain control of his fear and anger. These goons held no grudge against his ethnicity or supposed religious affiliation. They didn't care that he was a Jew, or even that he was an intellectual, although that was probably enough to have them curling their lips. No, he was a dead. That was enough. The new Secret Enemy in the belly of America, the Fifth Column for who knew what abominations. He was himself an abomination. His very being did dirt on life. He was a *refusnik* against the due punishment prescribed to mankind by pitiless Laws of Nature, and of Nature's God, so his refusal to remain dead was a blend of dirty joke and grotesque, outrageous treason to his species. Worse still, he thought with dizzy suppressed amusement, he hadn't paid his taxes. Death and taxes: yes, these were only the scourge of the living. Those laws would change. Perhaps they already had.

"Keep your hands where I can see them," the *Federale* said with flat menace. "Turn around. Face the wall. Assume the position."

"Position? What position?"

"Shut up, smartass. I won't tell you twice. Assume the position."

"I assume this position is something criminals know about. Not I, gentlemen. I can give you a quick lecture on the tactics of the Gestapo in the 1940s, if you like."

Strong fingers gripped him behind the left ear, dug in sharply. Excruciating pain, unbelievable. He thought he would faint. Probably not a mark on his flesh, he thought, stunned by the immediacy of this retribution. His arms were taken easily, crossed behind him, locked together. Klein was frogmarched into the corridor. He thought of screaming his lungs out, but there was no point. Dignity, he decided. Poise. A stately self-presence as he is taken to the tumbrel, the axe, the madhouse, the slaughterhouse.

Sylvie came out of her office, stared aghast.

"Please call that number I left with you and let them know. Tell them it's Mortuary Affairs," Klein said. Hard fingertips pressed again on the nerve plexus at his neck. Pain fired through him. He forced himself to add, gasping, "Let Professor Liu know that I won't be able to meet her for luncheon. Something's come up."

"Oh Jesus Christ Almighty fuck," cried the departmental manager, and ran back inside her office.

Jacoby walked at his side as he was taken from the cell. Klein had been confined for six days, stripped of his clothing and obliged to wear coarse orange prison garb, kept in isolation with no contact permitted with the outside world, personal or electronic. No TV or books, no computer, no writing materials. The lighting flickered irritably, surely by design, and a high-pitched whine made his teeth ache when he noticed it. He had decoupled from his situation, sunk in lethargy. Now he forced himself to pay attention, to deal with the urgencies of the living world.

"Am I going to be arraigned, Mr. Jacoby? If so, on what charge?"

Silence, other than the clack of the man's hard-heeled shoes on the concrete floor. Hushed slithering of Klein's slippers.

"I want to speak to a lawyer," he said, as he said every time a guard brought him a tray of barely edible food. "I have a constitutional right—"

Jacoby broke his silence. "You have no rights, Mr. Klein. You are a deceased person. I seriously suggest that you keep your mouth shut and respond only to questions put to you."

They entered a brightly lit room guarded by a stoical uniformed soldier with no obvious firearm but holding a sturdy baton, a fat LED Incapacitator at his belt. Seven seated men, no women, all warms, watched as Klein was pushed into a metal chair and his left wrist cuffed to a bolt. Jacoby said, "Gentlemen, this dead is Mr. Jorge Klein, a professor in the history department at UCLA, and an agent of the so-called Conclave of the Cold Towns."

"Professor mortuus," Klein said, "let us be accurate. And an agent of nothing but myself."

Astonishingly, Jacoby struck him hard across the face. "Quiet. You have been warned, Mr. Klein. You have no standing before this Board of Inquiry."

Robespierre, he thought. Yet again. *Terror is only justice that is prompt, severe and inflexible.* He moved his jaw. Not broken. In a loud clear voice he said, "Is one of these people my lawyer?"

Before Jacoby could hit him again, a burly fellow rose and came forward. "This is not a court of law, Mr. Klein, nor shall you have representation. You are here to answer our questions. It is the opinion of the Office of Mortuary Affairs that the rekindled have forfeited their legal status as citizens and indeed as human beings. Even as we speak, the Supreme Court—"

"Let us stay with the point, Colonel," said an older man at the back of the room.

"Quite right, General. The creature here is owed no explanations. Very well. Klein, you have visited sixteen of the Cold Towns in the last year, as well as traveling in the United Kingdom and Africa. In Tanzania, you engaged in furtive colloquy with your former wife, Sybille Klein, and her—"

"Sy*bille*," Klein said. "Not *Syb*ille. Already you're in danger of getting an 'F' for your report."

The burly man bared his yellow teeth. "In the mood for some quips, are we? That won't last long." He stroked a control panel on his wrist, and a large display opened on the wall at his left. The other men turned slightly to look at its tree diagram: names, locations of the Cold Towns scattered across the United States, estimates of untaxed net worth, links to the technological products flowing from the automatic factories of the deads. The figures for the fusion generators stood in a box at one side, impressive in both numbers of units and profits flowing from their lease. Klein's gaze moved steadily across the data as the man spoke, drawing out the connections. Links hinted at the torrents of information pouring in from the deep space telescopes, but it was apparent to Klein that these Jacobins had so far failed to unlock the source of the deads' accomplishments. He forced calm upon himself. This, it came to him in an instant of epiphany, was why he was here. It was the culmination of his program of highly visible advocacy. And he knew with cold clarity that he would be expunged the moment he had told them what they wished to learn. Well. He had been dead. He would be dead again. The entire cosmos was a long Death March toward obliteration.

A flunky had come forward, pushing a trolley laden with wireless instruments. Several hypodermics gleamed beside fat ampoules. He was deftly wired with contact points. All of this could be handled with microscopic probes, he thought, frightened but amused by the blatant theatrics. A line of colored tracer reports appeared across the top of the display.

"I screwed your fat Momma just now," he volunteered. A bright crimson bar lit up. "Just kidding," he added, and the bar switched to a yellowish-green.

"Not another word," Jacoby said in his ear, with menace.

"But I have so much to tell these gentlemen," Klein said airily. He entered a state of indifference and clarity. No doubt subtle synaptic changes dictated by his rekindled condition. "We have nothing to hide, after all. You just had to ask." The bar of light settled into a cheerful leafy green.

He unreeled it for them, the secret history. Klein knew himself to be an authority only on events and horrors a century gone, no expert at all in technology or the arcane of the sciences, but he knew how to tell a story, to hold captive a restive audience of teenaged students lacking interests in any topic beyond keg parties, good mood pills, sport, murderous stereo immersion games, and sex, sex, sex. He called upon these skills effortlessly, and for the most part held his captors spellbound, despite grumbles and occasional shouts of "Bull*shit!*"

Here is the last of the great NASA programs before the Grim Reset devaluation of the globe's currency slashed away 99 percent of each dollar: the skein of lensed cubesats flung out above the ecliptic to catch light a million, a billion, thirteen billion years old. Heroic and abandoned, processing the noise of deep space, reorienting its autonomic gaze like a star puppy hunting quail. The faint signal—not from a nearby star like the red dwarf Gliese 876 or HD 28185 or Upsilon Andromedae A, whose giant worlds in the habitable zone might hold Earthlike moons, but an unknown world in the nearby galaxy Andromeda, two million lightyears distant. The pulse, the stream, the beat of not just life but intelligence—consciousness! Minds impossibly old, by human standards—sending out their messages from a history more ancient now, if they survived, than the earlier upright ancestor of *Homo sapiens.* And tracked now not by a government, not by a consortium of politically funded academics, but by fanboy and fangirl billionaires, high-technology mavens, hundreds of millions each even after the Reset. Canny dreamers whose disciplines were, as if by magic or cosmic design, precisely fitted to unlocking the intelligible mysteries coded into the signal from Andromeda: coders and decoders, cypherpunks, cold-fusion fans, immensely rich game builders, Übergeeks, do-it-yourself connectomists looking for the tricks of enhancement and immortality that random mutations had never found.

A storm of angry incredulity broke finally over his head.

"Impossible! Maybe there's a signal, but nobody could decode that torrent so quickly."

"And if they did, what would they get? The *Weltbild* of silicon blobs! Not even that—no Rosetta Stone!"

"Right. What kind of ethnocentric wet-dream is this?"

Klein waited until they calmed down. "Look at me," he said. "Do I look like the product of any previous human science?"

"You look like something out of the nightmares of mankind," one of them cried in an agonized tone. "You look like a fucking vampire!"

Well. For the moment he had lost the argument. But he had planted a seed. They would water it with their own spleen and the enriched blood of his fellow deads, almost certainly his own blood, and that of Mi-Yun, Francine, Tom, the Guidefathers across the country, sure to be seized at gun and gas and bomb-point and incarcerated, probably murdered. Sybille, and her dilettante crew. Poor damned Dolorosa, wherever he was scurrying these days. But the enemy could not win. The warms could not win this war they were unleashing on the deads. Klein swore that to himself.

"Take this creature back to his cell," the Mortuary Affairs chieftain said. "We have work to do, gentlemen."

He was charged with no crime. No attorney ever heard from him. His family, he supposed, were informed of his accidental death, perhaps on the Kilimanjaro climb. People wept, no doubt, or shrugged. He sat on the hard bed and thought of the child he might have fathered after all with Sybille, the placid life they might have shared had she not perished from idiopathic pulmonary hypertension, had he not pestered her after her rekindling like a love-poisoned swain, and been poisoned himself in turn, fatally, by her bored crew. But he had been brought back, remade, a kind of metaphysical Philoctetes bearing the stench of his change, his rekindling, into the appalled and furious nostrils of his parent species. Days passed. Weeks passed. Months. It was a nothingness fit for a dead man.

In late February, he was taken to a place of execration, where an experimental biostasis unit awaited him. Work stolen from the deads, without doubt. His clothes were stripped from his waxy flesh. Instruments pierced his body. Not Philoctetes now but Saint Sebastian.

"Tell me what's happened to my colleagues? My friends? Have the Cold Towns been destroyed?"

149

"Hold your tongue."

An official of the Office came forward.

"You are an enemy of the State, and more crucially of the entire species of Humankind. You willfully hid knowledge that might have advanced the men and women of your nation by thousands of years. Fortunately for you, we are not a vengeful people. This is a Christian nation. Your sentence is extreme rendition, not death but exile. Jorge Amadeus Kline, you are to be exiled into the future for a period of decontamination not less than one century in duration. May God have mercy on what passes for your soul."

As he screamed, they put him into the chamber. A nurse attached a tube to the catheter in his neck. The face loomed above him, wavered, went away. Klein was gone.

Eight

O the mind, mind has mountains; cliffs of fall
Frightful, sheer, no-man-fathomed. Hold them cheap
May who ne'er hung there. Nor does long our small
Durance deal with that steep or deep. Here! creep,
Wretch, under a comfort serves in a whirlwind: all
Life death does end and each day dies with sleep.

Gerard Manley Hopkins, "Mind Has Mountains"

Was this death? Was it dream? Was it some cheapjack gamer fantasy he had been plugged into, solace of a kind in his century of incarceration? He drowned. Or was he surfacing from the deeps? *Thalassa! Thalassa!* The sea! The sea! The wild cries of Xenophon's men, at the end of this great and terrible march upcountry, sighting the Black Sea. The black endless sea of deep space. No sibilants in that cry from Hellene throats and tongues, in ancient Greek: *The latter! The latter!* That dry scholarly jest, he'd heard it as a student of history from his pretty fellow student. Was her name...Genevieve? Jennifer? Simply Jenny? Should it be spelled *Thalatta* or *Thalassa*? Why, the latter. All Greek to me, Jorge Klein had muttered (mussered?) with a grin. What is this nonsense chasing through his gelid, his sluggish mind? Cliffs of fall. Frightful, sheer. The sea, the sea! Is this hypnogogic or hypnopompic fancy? He cannot put his finger on it. He cannot put his finger on anything. He is entirely paralyzed. Dies with sleep. Drowning. Dies—

He was dead and stilled. The anguish of it terrified him.
Again a voice cried loudly: "Awaken, Klein! Behold your child!"

Klein convulsed out of death's sleep to some state more piercing, more clarified, than the distanced alertness of the dead. A legged fish, nearly weightless, he kicked in air. I'm on a free trajectory spacecraft, he told himself. Or a Lagrange station. Faces peered at him. A high priest of himself loomed, clad in ceremonial silk embroidered with the raw nerves of a flayed human body. Klein shuddered.

Figures tussled for a view of their divinity, their maker and destroyer, rekindled again from the deeper death. Three bald youths, struttish but dutiful, faces like warrior fiends, brandished meter-long scrolls of gold and jade. In tattered remnants of silk, an old man huddled closer. His lips moved in senile supplication. Two young women struggled to hide awed giggles behind cowls torn from silvery insulation. Klein blinked, cursing. The place was a shambles. A young woman's face came into focus, an Asian face, pretty, desecrated with rusted wire and small vivid points of light. Her full breasts were bared in the prideful modesty of a Primipara Mother. She held forth a small struggling bundle.

"The child of death!" cried the priest, reaching down from his floating eminence to unswaddle the tiny infant. "Behold !" Her discarded clothing hung free, tugged by stray air currents. Klein blenched as his eyes rose to the baby's face. Her features were a delicious blend of mother and father. She squalled: passion suffused her small cheeks and forehead. His daughter, beyond question. What madness had he done in death? It was forbidden. But by whose law? Damn their prohibitions and strictures!

"August Personage!" bellowed the gathering of his shabby worshipers. "Welcome back to the life of the dead!"

"Take the daughter of your loins, Lord!" the priest urged. Klein shook his head in repudiation. "Your beloved child! Prophesied from time out of time."

Very well; renewed living death. Reluctantly, impelled by a kind of ancient reverence, Klein held out his hands and took the baby's weightlessness, glanced again at her milky features, murmured her name as the devotees howled and babbled in holy delight.

"Peach Tree of Immortality," he said softly. She should have been male, his son and heir, Heavenly Master of the Dawn of Jorge Klein of the Golden Door. For a moment, catching himself, he suspected treachery, imposture. But his blood sang with hers. This was his child.

"Tree! Sacred Tree! Child of Klein!" screamed the last of his believers.

152

Concussion struck the vessel. The faithful squealed and scrambled, fleeing backward out of the cramped cabin. Metallic but controlled, a rough voice announced from an ancient ambient system: "Hull breach. An armed vessel attacks. All hands! All hands!"

Explosions thumped terrifyingly, transmitted through the hull. Klein stared about him, clutching the baby. The young Queen-Mother reached for her daughter, desperate, face distorted. Her name was...was...Struck again and again by the enemy weapons, the ruined starcraft jolted, ringing like a bell. Milk leaped from Mi-Yun's naked nipples, opalescent globules that hung in the sweat-reeking air like pearls.

"What vessel assails us?" the priest demanded of the ambient. He was calm, no longer ludicrous in vile robes.

Again a crash. "It appears to be...a ship of Earth."

Klein stared. The warms? In an instant, his torpor was flung from him, and with it every vestige of learned sophistication, acquired so painfully in a long lifetime and deadtime of intensely diligent study in the ways of human civilization. He raged like a wild beast in a cage, yet careful in his fury of the baby against his shirtless chest, wrathful.

"The child," cried Queen-Mother Mi-Yun, tearing at his arms with nails that left bloodless tracks down his flesh. "Put down my baby!"

Klein ignored pain and cries alike. He drew his daughter against his breast, and crossed to the tangle locus. "Send me to their ship," he said. Terrified, the technician matched parameters and activated the entanglement field. Klein transitioned instantly into the enemy vessel.

Glancing at him without visible surprise, a dead woman smiled coolly with eyes blue as Californian summer skies. She sat upright but utterly relaxed in her acceleration chair on the bridge, clad in the crisp whites of a spacecraft commander. Nobody else was on the bridge. He listened to her controlled breathing, and his own, and the baby's steady heart beat. Nothing else but machinery. They were alone on the great vessel.

"Jorge," she said. Sybille's voice was crushed mint on chilled glass. "A daddy now, I see. How touching."

Convulsion. Confusion. Nightmare, nothing but a nightmare. Muddled thoughts in a blue funk.

"Sir. Sir. Mr. Klein. Are you fully awake, sir?"

And his full consciousness switched on, like a searchlight. He sat up. A small room with curved walls, pale peach, air humming. A young man in the classic garb of an orderly watched him, cautiously. A warm. A warm! So. They had brought him back up from his purging, his term of punishment, his warehousing. A century come and gone on a calendar, lost to him forever. Klein twitched his muscles, sat up without a pang, swung his legs over the side of what appeared to be an operating table.

"I'm feeling surprising well, actually." He touched his neck, regarded his arms. Tubes gone, no apparent scars. Klein turned his back on the orderly, put his hands on the edge of the table and did several squats. He felt terrific. Light on the soles of his feet. Vim and vigor, with a faint tremor that seemed to spread outward into the floor itself. Well, this was the future, after all, home of fantastic progress. His thoughts darkened immediately. The prison gates would open, even in the best of all possible worlds, and he'd be released into a world as a stranger and afraid, sundered by a hundred years from all he knew. Cold seized him, and he fell forward, pressed hard, gripping the table's padded edge. "No, no," he said sharply, waving away the orderly (or cryo-technician? A doctor perhaps?). "Give me a moment." He breathed slowly. "So we're halfway through the twenty-second century."

"No, sir. Really, I'd feel happier if you'd lie down again for a moment."

Grumbling, Klein did so. The electrostatic field he associated with Sybille's funeral lifted him smoothly, like rocking gently in air. Not, in this case, an antinecrotic, he supposed. Was there the same tang of jasmine? His impoverished nostrils could not discern subtle odors.

"Thank you. Sir, you have been released from suspension early. It is now a little more than 43 years after your interment."

That was a jolt. Klein did hasty calculations. So: 2083. Chances were, though, that his brother in-law-Moshe would have succumbed to old age, perhaps to death. Hester? She might still be alive. Or would they, too, despite their early prejudice, turn to rekindling? He pushed himself up again on his elbows.

"Who authorized this?"

"The Committee of the Party for Unification," the orderly said somewhat piously. "Sir, all your questions will be answered in a—"

A man in dark blue military uniform came into the room, a hard-faced fellow perhaps in his late fifties. His features seemed oddly familiar. Moshe? No, no. The orderly saluted and made himself scarce. Surely not—

"Jorge Klein," the man said, and his lined face made a smile as his hand reached across in a firm grip. "Uncle Jorge, I mean."

"Eli! Eliezer! My god, boy. You're older than I am!"

"Physiologically, yes. While you've been snoring on your back, my associates and I have been trying to hold the world together."

"There's a war, I suppose." Klein felt his lips twist.

"All the possible wars at once," Solomon said. He dragged over a stool, reached into his breast pocket for gum, offered a stick to Klein, who shook his head, appalled and amused. "Worst of all, the war between the quick and the deads."

"Christ. It really did come to that, then." He stared at the man's clenched jaw, powerful hands. "But you're a warm yourself, Eli. Am I to be executed after all?"

"On the contrary. My faction is opposed to retribution against the rekindled at large. They were hardly responsible for the actions of the madmen among them. We're reviving all the imprisoned—"

"Retribution?" Klein was taken aback. "*We* were the victims, Eli, from day one. Sybille was killed in the bombing of Zion Cold Town. You can't possibly believe that."

"Shut up, Klein." Solomon stood, face flushed. "You don't know what you're talking about. How could you possibly offer a germane opinion?"

"Don't shout at me, Eliezer." Klein forced himself to take a breath. "I'm sorry—Mr. Solomon. What's your rank, anyway?"

The man ignored him, voice deepening in fury. "You know nothing of the hyperkinetic rock that smashed Jerusalem. Here, look at what your people did to mine. And to all the others."

A wall stereo display activated, opening its imaginary space into echoing depths. For a moment, Klein was dizzied; the protocols of presentation were unfamiliar. Images, captions, a muted voice-over that Solomon silenced. Temple Mount—Har haBáyith, the

Haram Ash-Sharif—key disputed holy ground of Judaism and Islam, smashed into ruin by a blazing infalling rock the size of a hill. St. Peter's Papal Basilica, marvel of art and devotion, majestic Renaissance triumph of Michelangelo and a hundred other artists of genius, gone with the whole of Rome in a kinetic fireball. The Kaaba in the Grand Mosque, with its ancient meteoric Black Stone, obliterated by another ravening meteorite. A great Hindu temple to Lord Shiva, a thousand years old, hundreds of feet of brilliantly carved granite, expunged. The Temple of the Latter Day Saints. Image after brilliant archival image, spliced with the burning things in the sky caught from below, from the screaming distance, from sharp-eyed satellites.

"The Hajar-e-Aswad II that wiped out Mecca. The Petrus impactor on Rome. All the great holy places of the world. Rajarajeswaram, India's largest Hindu temple. Lhasa. Salt Lake City. Smashed into craters of glass and dust by targeted rocks flung down by deads in lunar orbit. Murder and desecration. The worst assault on people of faith since—"

You see, I don't care, Klein thought. He had a distant academic interest in how this global apocalypse, this new Holocaust, might work itself out, and from what disputed beginnings it had arisen, but these impassioned words and fearful images seemed to him altogether detached from his own reality.

"You think the deads are opposed to religion? Violently opposed?"

"Aren't you?"

"Violently? No, absolutely not."

"You see the evidence there."

"No. Only evidence of violence, not of dead involvement. Why should we go to such absurd lengths? Such effort? You simply don't get it, Eli. The deads don't care."

He waved his hand back and forth, finally put it on his nephew's arm.

"Eliezer. Listen to me. Yes, this is terrible, but so was the Black Death. So were the millions dead in Cambodia and China. So was the Holocaust, and we are both tied to that in our bone and gristle, but listen to me: it doesn't matter. Not to me."

Eliezer Solomon was speechless with disbelief and then with outrage. "You cannot begin—"

156

"You're right, Eli, I can't, What I want to know is much more immediate. What news of your parents? Are they alive? What of the deads I lived with? Sybille you yourself knew, but there were others. A woman named Mi-Yun, another named Francine. A man called Tom." Did they mean anything to him, those deads, in this wasteland of noise and nothingness? No, not truly. But he had to ask.

"Your sister Hester and my dad were in Israel, in Tel-Aviv, when Jerusalem and much more was destroyed from space. Gone, gone, with millions of Jews."

"And how many Arabs? A million? Are they at each other's throats? Or does everyone blame the deads?"

"All the possible wars, I told you. Yes, the dead are blamed by the intelligentsia, because you are the masters of advanced technology. Only your fusion systems could have mobilized asteroids and hurled them at the Earth like David's rock from a sling. But the great masses curse their favorite enemies and heretics, and martyrs' blood is shed on all sides. As was planned, I am certain of it." Solomon sat down again, wiped his face with a handkerchief. "Sybille Klein has been deaccessioned. I did a search before I came down here. I knew you'd want to know. The others, no, their names are not familiar. I imagine they, too, are gone. That's why we've chosen to save you and the rest, Jorge. You are an endangered species, you deads. An experiment that was…cut short. Well, not if we can help it. I must warn you, you'll be placed back in suspension when we get to our destination."

What? What? Instant understanding, then. The lightness against his muscles, the tremor at the edge of detection in the floor.

"We're in space."

"Yes, I thought you'd been told."

"Where?"

"Halfway to Mars, at point nine gees. One more day. Then we will put you in protective custody. Biostasis is a lot safer. You'll complete your sentence. The future might revile you, but they might find some reason for retaining you."

"No release program, then. No generous reconciliation with the warm Master Race."

Eliezer Solomon, soldier, went to the door. His face was a cold mask.

157

"*You* are the Master Race, Jorge. You rekindled. And it looks as if you've met the usual fate of Masters." He said with finality, "I'll never see you again. Goodbye."

Klein lowered his eyes. All of them dead, then, deader than dead. Deaccessioned! Filthy, banal euphemism. Or smashed like vermin. Suddenly he felt very tired and tremendously hungry. "Yes, goodbye, Eli." But when he raised his head his nephew was gone, and the orderly was back, fussing.

Was this memory? Was it dream? Drowning Klein fought for consciousness, air, sanity—

Stench of human suffering, of his own decaying flesh. Shivering, filthy, Klein shuffled into the moon-lit darkness from the hateful wooden barracks he shared with a dozen other men, not all of them Jews. Three in the morning again. Nothing to drink for an hour, then that disgusting bitter coffee, all he'd get for five o'clock breakfast. Hours of crippling labor hauling rocks and manure before lunch, weak soup, hardly enough to make you crap. A young Schutzstaffel officer with the detestable lightning runes on the collar of his neat, clean uniform, shouting at some wretched miscreant. From a barracks separate from the Jews, a swaggering "camp elder" came to deliver suitable punishment. The Jews cringed away from him; Klein cowered, tried to hide from the criminal's gaze. A rapist and murderer, Heinz Klausner was head Capo, boss of the scum "barracks police." Klein failed to evade the man's eyes. The prick came striding over in his new green trousers, his tall leather boots catching the pale light of the moon, seized Klein by his own ragged collar. "Slacking again, you creature," he shouted. They had a miraculous power to find ire within themselves, for their own satisfaction and the enjoyment of the watching SS thugs. He slapped Klein hard, yelling abuse. Nobody came to his aid. Klein fell, was hauled up. The SS officer stepped forward. "Here, men, we have a good 'boxing sack.' Time to sharpen your fighting skills." Piss ran down Klein's legs. Let me go, Lord, he prayed. Let me die now. Poor Chaim Shustack, burliest and strongest of the remaining Jewish prisoners, was pulled forward. "Hold the creature up, you vermin." I'm sorry, I'm sorry, Chaim's eyes told him. Here came Klausner's boot, swung smashingly into his left knee. He sagged, fell forward. Shustack heaved at his right arm, kept him from falling. Another SS thug found a heavy stick, struck him in the mouth. His teeth splintered. Agony.

More kicks. His balls! Cramping in his abdomen, muscles rigid. He could not breathe. Give me death, give me death.

This time he awoke instantly.

The pseudo-memory of his post-biostasis dream clung like a rancid film.

Oh. Oh. Oh.

Gasping, he surged up, flung himself from the catafalque. Hands of attendants reached in alarm to prevent him from falling, but Klein was on his hands and knees, staring wildly, seeking a place to hide. His broken mouth! His ribs! His brutalized balls! Crawling from the light, cowering beneath the floating catafalque, he covered his head, touched his tender mouth. His teeth were intact. Wait, wait. No aching in his balls, no contusions or fractures. Why would they impose this horror upon him? He crept out into the large green room, watched by two women and a man. They seemed concerned. Yes, yes, a fantasy, that was all. Something he'd imposed upon himself, no doubt. His specialty study, after all, corroding the depths of his unconscious, the Nazi era of the twentieth. Or some residual guilt. For what? It had not been he who bombed those so-called holy places, smashing them from space.

But that must have happened decades ago. He was…on…Mars? No, the gravity was wrong. Earthlike. Exactly Earthlike. Seeking some scrap of dignity, he got to his feet.

"Dead sir," said an attendant, "du need not fear us."

"No," he said. They were warms, but something had changed in them, some change deep and strange. He covered his face for a moment of consolidation. No beard. They had shaved him, depilated him. Patting, probing, he found a fine thick bush of hair on his scalp, hanging down his neck, like the very non-military coiffure of the male attendant. "All right. Very well. Where is this place? What is the date?"

"Many passed by. No know exactamund. Where is your departure date? What jahr?"

Klein stared. "How could you not know? I was in a machine, a biostasis chamber, they called it. Isn't there a…a calendar? A data display? A small rectangle with changing numbers in red light or something?"

"So sorry, Meister Dead. No access to biostationary records, all lost in the Disruption."

The Smash-Up, yes. All the possible wars. Klein groaned. The stupidity of it all. He could not believe it had been occasioned solely by resentment of the rekindling process, envy for what its beneficiaries had created. Who was to say that the deads were not a scapegoat after all? Yet surely the power source required to shunt whole asteroids from orbit and target them at select sites on Earth—that had to be the technology of the Conclave, or some heretical splinter group. He groaned again.

"You must have some idea. Decades? Centuries?"

"Hundreds jahren, certes." The others nodded their speculative agreement. "Two hundred. Three." A hand wave.

Klein sank into a gray place.

The woman with streaks in her dark cropped hair was asking him meaningless questions. "Which was your god? Scuzi, that is your gog. And magog."

"No god, no gog," he said bleakly. "Magog, for sure. He tore up the world, last time I was there."

They did not grasp his allusion, shrugged at each other. "Your name, good being? Some records remain, we might find more on your interrupted life course."

"Call me Ishi," he said bitterly.

"Ah!" The man was delighted. "Old remnant document. 'Call me Ishmael.'"

"Close, but no biscuit," Klein said. That dreadful dream. It could have been his grandfather's life and pitiless death, except that his family had escaped the iron heel in time. "Ishi was the last member of the Yahi, and they were the last surviving sept of the Californian Yana people. Back at the start of the twentieth. Taken in hand by Kroeber and Waterman. You don't want to know about this."

"A jest, a pun, a play of nominalism! Most delightful!" This second young woman was a vivid redhead, curls piled up on curls. Her body was succulent, clad in bright chrome-yellow. Looking at her, he felt nothing.

"And what am I to call you people?"

The man smiled sunnily. "I, Jesus." Hay-Zeus. The dark haired woman said, "I, Mary." With the cutest little bow, the girl, the young woman, told him, "I, Joseph."

Klein burst out laughing. "You're shitting me."

"Assuredly not, sir. We adopt these nominations from your mystery book, to render du the more at ease."

"It hasn't worked. For one thing, Joseph is a man's name."

The redhead cocked her head like a puzzled Pomeranian. "Names have no gender, sire. But we still await your true nomenclature."

"Jorge Klein," he said. "Klein is my surname."

"Ah, so! Sir Klein!"

"No, no, just Klein. Never mind." These ninnies were as much fun as a barrel of eels. "And you, you're what we termed warms, back in my day. Whenever that was."

"Not especially close to identical," the man told him. "We have the augments, as do all. All but the deads, of whom there are, du know, hardly no more no more. Du are our precious, however contemptible."

Rekindling, they explained, was now seen as a frightful horror, worse than foot-binding or genital mutilation, worse even than lobotomy.

"They gave some man a Nobel prize for inventing lobotomy, you know," Klein said, mouth twisted. "Or probably you don't."

"It is noway noble to cut open a head or poke through the eye, ruining the tissues. There was awards for this barbarity?"

"Only the one," Klein reassured him. "I believe it was revoked."

"Du have one of these Noble Prizes?"

"I could have been a contender," Klein said.

"But it was done to du, speaking in the manner of a synecdoche. Or mayhap a metonymy."

Chill through his dead flesh. "What? What?" Without intention, his hands again went at once to his head, probing, pressing his eyes and the sockets holding them. "You're lying."

"For no reason would we, sir Ishi. Du are a dead. Du suffered the notorious 'drying out' following your revival."

"Yes. We all did. Part of the procedure. It's a metaphor. Quite possibly it's a synecdoche, or mayhap a metonymy. Moths and butterflies. Do you have them now? Have all the beasts been exterminated on Earth? They creep from their pupas and cocoons, altogether changed, wet with the slime of transformation. They dry out. Simile with us." His tongue caught. He realized that despite his long, long

161

sleep (how long? How long?), he was exhausted. Carefully, he said, "I mean similarly."

"No, no, for what precedes drying? Why, washing. The washing of the brain. Du was programmed like an old clanker robot, sir."

"What? Nonsense." Oh Christ. Oh my god.

"Yes, du see, your language menus reset from without. How to fast dead talk. Prohibitions on sexuality. No children. Too large a population otherwise. Very slick. Now we all do that fast talk, du might have noticed, but with our optional implants. Us warms are enhanced, see it?"

It crushed his spirit. For these years since his rekindling, meaninglessness had been his companion, but this was intolerable, unsustainable. He sagged, and the bright woman caught him under the right arm. He flinched away (the Capo! The Jew-killer!), then let her ease him back on his catafalque. The world, the worlds, had shrunk to a series of small clean well-lighted hospital recovery rooms. So he was not just dead, he was an automaton. Pre-programmed for the long empty life of a dead. Drowning again, this time awake. He sought for something to cling to.

"But the war is over?" he said, and heard an unaccustomed plaintive note in his voice. "The warms and the dead are at peace once more?"

All three laughed. "Oh, no no," Jesus said "By no means, Mr. Ishi. Mr. Klein. Such enmity is not so easily quelled." The man took up his hand. "But we have great hopes for du, sir. We ask du to intervene with the voices from Andromeda nebula." He blinked. "Scuzi, galaxy."

But Klein was not listening. A child. He was not sterile, then. Not impotent. Not a sexless thing. Or if he was, it was a constraint imposed upon him by the Guidefathers and the sons of bitches running the Conclave. He might break free. He might father a daughter, or a son. If the beings from Andromeda permitted it. For surely they were the puppet masters. Whoever they were. Whatever. He whirled in gray interior space, groped for meaning, for sense, for purpose.

"Voices," he said, then. "What voices? How could we understand aliens?" It had always been the sticking point. Claims of cyphering, hypercomputers, Gödel coding—none of it was ultimately persuasive. *Eppur si muove.* And yet it moves. We have the technology.

"Not all alien," said Joseph. "Some of them are human voices, po-jąć? From the future."

And theatrically, operatically, a tremendous gonging strikes the air, slams the floor. Those fantastical images of bombardment and carnage flare again in Klein's mind. His daughter Tree.

"We're under attack," Mary said, and the three warms went into a huddle. No doubt bolts of energy pulsed between their brains, their rewired neurons, and every other warm in the building. Another immense shock flung them off their feet. The three rolled like circus acrobats, were on their toes in moments. Klein lay where he had fallen, rubbing his bruised elbow.

"Where are we?" he said with what he considered admirable restraint. "And who's trying to kill us?"

They looked at him fishily. "Approaching the Andromeda vinculum mouth, du did not dig this? The precise location for your undertaking. To speak for all, as a relict of the *evenements*."

Klein closed his eyes. He felt very old and useless.

"So I'm still on a spaceship. An attack ship under fire off the shoulder of Orion, I suppose."

Joseph placed a comforting hand on his cheek. "Nobody transports so far as yet. We remain above the ecliptic, beyond the Oort Cloud."

"So who the hell is firing on us?"

"Why, can't you pursue elementary logic, sir Klein? Your last companionables, obviously. The deads on board the pioneer starship *Tell Me Not, In Mournful Numbers*, stationed at the vinculum. Now we must answer that message with one less harmful. When they learn that you are with us, they shall abandon their fusillade, certes." She shut her eyes, reached with her left hand for Mary and her right for Jesus. The gravity switched off, and they ascended in a Coriolis curve from the rolling deck, with Klein, like a small flock of wingless angels.

Deep space was truly black, and through the unreflecting bubble the Milky Way was a wide, thick band of brightness. In every direction, points of gemlike light. Klein had expected to find his vision adjusted to the faint interior illumination of the transfer bubble—that miracle of field forces centuries in advance of his own lost time—but somehow the clarity was electrifying. Behind him, the complex shape of the warms' vessel was itself a dozen curved mirrors flinging back starlight. Ahead, the starship of the deads (or was it a blended crew of the dead and the quick? he could not be sure) resembled a finless fish, smooth as black ice in the blackness, rimmed by forces that pulsed almost fast enough to make an uninterrupted glow. And beyond that enormous vehicle, a hanging indigo shape like the manifestation of a tesseract, a rotating impossible object in five or six or thirteen dimensions: the throat of the vinculum created two million years ago by the beings in Andromeda.

It is a phallus, Klein thought. Readying itself to plunge into the yoni of the vinculum. How banal. How inevitable.

"So that thing is going to rocket into—"

"No no, no reaction forces. They use a method. Du would not understand."

Nettled, Klein said, "Just keep it simple."

"Oh, like a kinder learning, yes, very good. They employ a strong symplectic homeomorphism. With this—"

Klein gritted his teeth. "Simple, Joseph."

"But this is elementary. Your Hamiltonian spaceology on its own isotopies are generalized to an intrinsic symplectic topology on the space of symplectic isotopies, obviously." The young woman gazed at him guilelessly in the darkness, her features limned by starlight. "By coupling to the—"

"Stop," Klein said. "Just stop."

Abruptly a glistening bubble came from the star-strewn darkness, hesitated athwart their own, merged. Klein's ears popped. Four humans stepped forward. One of them he knew at once, hardly changed by the centuries. Perhaps he had slept in stasis as well. Yet was there not an added quality of gravitas to the man, a sense of calm self-worth as he stepped forward and took Klein's hand?

"Hi. We're gonna take a little trip. You up for that, doc?" Dolorosa said, and grinned like an avuncular rodent.

Huffing out a cough of amusement, Klein said, "You advised me rather a long time ago not to ask deads a direct question."

"Things change, Klein. Things change."

That, too, echoed like some refrain from his lost history. The little Customs man, was it? Barwani. Tags of who he had been, his ignorance, his hopeless and stupid obsession, clung like barnacles washed by brackish waters. Things change. Yet now that he looked at the dead standing beside Dolorosa, he realized with a jolt how utterly that was true.

"Mi-Yun," he said. "They'd told me you were—"

"Deaxed? Not all of us. Who were the ones you knew? Francine, perhaps? Tom? Those were deaccessioned during the crisis. Didn't you have a wife once? Gone also. Quite a few of us survived, though, as you see. Let me introduce you to representatives of our crew. This is—"

The names of the warms fell into his ears, and he let them slip away. He went through to their section of the conjoined bubble.

"Goodbye, goodbye, goodbye, sir Klein. Carry our wishes to the future, to Andromeda. Well faring!"

And falling into the blackness, toward the phallic fish, the ichthyphallic starship. He sniggered. Too much, too much. Another galaxy! Rhodomontades of Wagner, Beethoven, Carl Maria von Weber, for Christ sakes, he needed Teutonic bombast again. Was he embarking on the Flying Dutchman? Fated to wander the lonely cosmos for eternity, dead, dead, dead, dead?

"Come on, old fellow," Dolorosa was saying. Their bubble had passed now into the belly of the beast. Busy crew went by with no great evidence of curiosity. In an elevator they ascended to an expanse Klein took to be the control center, or perhaps merely an entertainment alcove, two men and a woman on padded chairs, signally bare of consoles and keypads and swipe bars. Augmented warms, he reminded himself. No doubt they fly this thing by thought, by the flight of entangled electrons from brain to brain to picotechnological hypercomputer navigation systems. He halted.

"This is the commander of the Andromeda mission," Dolorosa said. "Captain Lucius Olanrewaju."

"Excuse me, Captain," Klein said, the words tight between his teeth. He was angry, angry, and this unaccustomed access of emotion seemed beyond his power to contain it. "This is not the moment," he ground out. "Take me away, please."

Mi-Yun, the changed Mi-Yun, understood at once. Murmuring to the warms, who smiled, bobbed their machine-laden heads, she departed gracefully with Klein, leaving Dolorosa to follow after them, his glance sardonic.

"How long will this trip take?" Klein asked her in the passageway. Two million years in biostasis? He thought. The dreams, the terrible dreams. That prospect was intolerable. Yet to remain awake and deathless for such eons…Worse still.

"Perhaps a millennium," Mi-Yun told him. "It will be painless, Jorge."

"And you wanted me…why?"

"You know why," Dolorosa said. "This was your vocation. You are to be the Apostle. The Ambassador."

"To the warms, Jamal Hakim said."

"Not only to them. To the aliens of Andromeda. They're waiting for you, sport."

"How can they know anything about me? How can *you* know anything about *them*?"

"You're muddled in the old errors," Mi-Yun said. "We know better now. Causality is tangled, entangled. Strictly, you see, there is no causality, only correlation."

Stupid abstractions. But yes, finally everything was an abstraction. Empty circularity. This never-ending emptiness, ruin. Not even yearning, not even disgust. Mi-Yun mistook his blank stare for intellectual engagement. She added, "It is the Shoup Scholium. Quantum entropy showed that measurement is a unitary three-interaction. No collapse, no fundamental randomness. Influence is equal between past and future, as perceived by us." Again he drifted away. Superposition, entanglement, measurement, locality, causality.

"Yes, Mi-Yun, whatever you say. I will do as you require, but on one condition."

The two deads, paused, watched him carefully. Did they know already? If past and future were paths one could travel in either direction, they might well have knowledge of his perverse desire. But their expressions conveyed neither revulsion nor excitement. Dolorosa was a scofflaw of old, he might raise no objection. But Mi-Yun—

"I want a child," he told them.

166

"You know that's impossible. The physiology—"

"I'm not taking about fucking and carrying a child in utero. Now that I find you here, waiting for me, I wish you to be the child's mother, Mi-Yun. Cells from each of us, reverted skin cells, they were doing this with mammals back in the 21st century."

She lifted her eyes to the left. She was augmented, as he'd suspected, searching the same grand and gnarly information spaces as the warms. "Induced Pluripotent Stem Cells," she said, nodding. "Primordial oocyte and spermatozoa precursors generated from— But our bodies are changed, Jorge. We are not strictly human. There is no reason to suppose that this could work."

"Surely this ship has biomedical equipment."

"Of course, but what you're asking is illegal and immoral." She regarded him with growing dismay. "You expect me to be the donor."

"Why not? Why not? You plan a voyage of two million lightyears, surely you don't balk at essaying parenthood?"

Mi-Yun's face showed agonized indecision. "And if I do this thing?"

"Why, then, call me Spock. Ambassador Spock," said Jorge Klein, raising his right hand in an ancient, long-forgotten salute, ironic twinned fingers raised to starboard and port. "Die long and prosper."

Nine

We are imprisoned in the realm of life, like a sailor on his tiny boat, on an infinite ocean.

Anna Freud

And again awakens, this time from no dreams he can recall. A thousand years into the future. The machines newly placed within his cranium as he slept tell him his location in the Andromeda galaxy, in a star battle cruiser warped there by an arcwise homeomorphism, its complement blended of the quick and the dead.

Tell him that he has been remade once more.

Stepping from the cool medical catafalque, his naked flesh maggot pale but in peak postmortem condition, Jorge Klein knows instantly, and with no need to search his declarative memory, these things and many more: That a millennium, yes, has passed as he lay immobile, tended by guardian machines, not merely dead but comatose. That he is aboard the battle cruiser *Tell Me Not, In Mournful Numbers* (and that it emerged from a transport vortex ninety-three minutes earlier, and is now decelerating at 50 gravities from light speed, that its complement is 1019 humans, and, irrelevantly, that the number 1019 is prime). That its destination is the G0 star Longer Baseline Galactic Survey 2374b39 in the Andromeda galaxy. That the war between the quick and the dead continues in fits and starts, fragmented across centuries, threatening ruin and extinction to both. That his illicit daughter, built from his codons and Mi-Yun's, nurtured in an artificial uterus, sleeps in biostasis, like the baby she is, three decks below. And, above all, in this cascade of immanent knowingness, that some grievous change has been wrought upon him. Within him. Again.

168

In a greater access of passion than his condition has permitted him for a thousand years, he speaks his unfamiliar rage to the empty room, "You bastards. You have *augmented* me! Against my express instruction."

A man stands before him. A holographic image, a stereo, a sentimental record of the lost past? But no, his hand reaches compassionately to touch Klein's brow. Dolorosa again, hair long, clad in a golden caftan. No longer the street rat, the snarling outsider. A man at home in his station. Which is, the augment tells Klein at once and without his striving for its access, Representative of the Conclave in Andromeda Space. Information has been flooding in from Earth, from Mars, from all the worlds of the Solar system, a thousand years of archived history, scientific advances, reports of the endless war. Flurries of art, new modes of music invented, abandoned as hackneyed, rediscovered, bypassed, overwhelmed by newer forms, and again and again. Through it all, the continuing augmentation of the warms, while the deads are all but paralyzed by their first adopter technological lock-in. Only the grim endurance of their indifference, their intrinsic aloofness, allows the rekindled to persist, even thrive. And of course the deads hold one important distinction: they don't die. Unless they are "deaccessioned."

All of this in stacked tree-indexed hierarchical order, a vast data cathedral rising in a triumphant architectonic surge into Klein's soul through his own augments, low-level as they are, as he now understands.

"Hey, man," says Dolorosa. He smiles in friendship, and his teeth are dazzlingly white and perfectly formed. If anything has been lost in this millennial chronicle of change, genemod dental implants has not been one. "I see you're back, and in fine fettle. Just cool it a mo, hey? The Droms want to talk to you, before we get to their world. Come with me, and we'll get you up to speed."

In a dry, rasping voice, Klein says, "My child. I want to see my baby."

"Sure, we can do that en route. Do you have a name for her yet? She's a little darlin', man."

Of course he has a name for her. "Eurydice," he says.

Dolorosa laughs out loud. "That'd do. You've brought her back from the dead. From two deads, hey." A beat. "Just don't look over your shoulder when—Never mind."

"You're right. There'd be endless jokes at her expense." He ponders as they walked through the twisted corridors of the battle cruiser. "Yael," he says. "For her grandmother."

"On your side, I guess. No say for Mi-Yun."

"She is my child," Klein says urgently. "Mine, mine."

"Keep your shirt on. Yai-el. Pretty name for a pretty gal. What's it mean?"

"Strength of God. Or maybe to ascend like a mountain goat. Everything's god to my people, even the goddam mountain goats." He thinks of his long exhausting climb up Kilimanjaro. Up this two million light-year staircase of stars and impossible constrained forces.

They pass through a gauzy veil of light, and enter a place of medical machines. "Here," Dolorosa says. "You can see her in the display."

Bitterly disappointed, Klein says, "I can't hold her? Not even a window to look through?"

"Her immune system is still having its final prep. But isn't she a cutie?"

The holo display above Yael's crib shows a sleeping infant with curly hair. Her eyes, with their enchanting epicanthic slant, will be dark as his, Klein thinks; as dark as grandmother's. And her hair already is black as her Korean mother's. He reaches despite himself into the depth field of the image, and meets nothing but air crossed by rays of light.

"I'll come back and get you soon," he whispers to his daughter. "I love you, little one."

As he turns away, reluctantly, following Dolorosa's tug at his sleeve, he feels tears leaking down his cheeks, and his narrow world, slowing fantastically from light speed, blurs and shivers.

Battle cruiser or not, this vessel seems to be run on a surprisingly relaxed basis. Warms and deads walk the passageways, doors slide open and shut, voices murmur. He hears no ship-wide announcements snapped from hidden speaker systems; no flashing red or green panels alert the crew to the status of the vessel. Perhaps such functions are delegated to the augments, all the complex background information vital to the running and survival of the craft somehow integrated into the silent activity of the flesh, like the body's automatic awareness of heat and cold, bright and dim, loud explosions, a fist swung toward the face, with responses mechanical and instantaneous. Would his own unsought implants bear the same warnings and requests? Perhaps so. Nobody stops him from entering the public spaces, but no door opens to private cabins. For an hour he prowls this way and that, building a slowly clarifying sense of the structure of this immense ship. In one room, apparently a dedicated place for dining, he finds warms eating and drinking, laughing a little but not raucously, chatting but not chattering. At an empty table he sits, suddenly weary, and after a time a man in a horizontally striped shirt and a jaunty black beret fetches him a plate of steaming spaghetti with a thick red fishy sauce. He sprinkles cheese across it, adds pepper, tastes. A piquant flavor. Is his sense of taste returning? It's true; his nostrils clear, as if for years he has been afflicted by a tiresome cold. Klein shovels the spaghetti marinara into his mouth, overwhelmed by the rediscovery of taste and appetite. Wine is poured, a rich red Cabernet. The plate is taken away. He places his head on his folded arms, overwhelmed, and drifts off.

He dreams that he is in República Argentina again, in the heart of Buenos Aires, leading a team of architects through the magnificent Edificio Kavanagh, its lofty Art Deco setbacks imploring the sky, clean in its towering concrete lines, brilliant with sunlight; it will become the first Cold Town outside the borders of the United States. The builders frown, mutter among themselves angrily. An affront! This classic building is one of the marvels of their city. It is not a mausoleum, a vertical catacomb, it is a home for the living, the warm. No, no, he protests; he tries to explain. It is his father and mother he addresses; their faces are flushed with anger. Who does he think he is? Little Hester cowers in her mother's skirts. Across the dining room in this high Westwood Plaza restaurant, the neo-Babylonian Hanging Gardens, he sees a lovely young woman enter, and Hester plucks at his sleeve. "She's perfect for you. She's your type, I swear." It is Mick Dongan's bony fingers grabbing at his jacket. "Her name is Sybille. She's from Zanzibar. Look, look, she's a dead, Klein, just like

171

you, the perfect choice." He groans in protest, and the hand is shaking his shoulder.

"This isn't really the place for a snooze," Mi-Yun tells him, gazing down. Her wise old face. Klein blinks, clears away the film of moisture from his eyes. It is not that she looks old. No new lines, no sinking of the cheeks, her dark eyes have not withdrawn within crêpey sockets, there's no desperate thinning of the lips. Yet she is changed profoundly. Has she been awake all these ten long centuries? Or just for the two or three hundred years beyond the catastrophic bombing of Jerusalem, Mecca, Rome, all the high places of faith and power and mad rivalrous bigotry? She picks up his limp hand. "Come on, my dear. You've had a hard transition. Let's go to bed."

She leads him down carpeted passageways to a large cabin, a suite really. They undress in the lowered light of softly glowing lamps, and she draws him beneath the sheets. Under her gentle ministrations, Jorge Klein relaxes, at last, tension easing, tight muscles yielding. They do not kiss; he does not stiffen, enter her; they make love in the way of the deads, touching lightly, placing their hands upon each other, the blooms of flowers brushing before a cool breeze.

Klein smiles, sighs, slips into sleep.

Ten

I did not think I was strong enough to retain for long a past that went back so far and that I bore within me so painfully. If time enough were allotted me to accomplish my work, I would not fail to mark it with the seal of Time, the idea imposed upon me with so much force: that humans are monsters occupying in time a habitation infinitely more significant than the restricted locations reserved for them in space, a place immeasurably extended because, touching widely separated epochs and the slow accretion of days upon days passed through, we stand like giants immersed in Time.

Marcel Proust, *Time Regained*

The world LBGS 2374b39c, third planet of its Andromedan star, turns below them into the light of its Sun as the battle cruiser goes on orbit. Captain Lucius Olanrewaju stands before the command deck's immense holo display. Klein is seated; in the last weeks of the ship's deceleration he has undertaken extensive briefings, and awaits his removal to the surface. The planet is a golden-red haze of dust, Mars inflated to the diameter of the Earth, plus eleven percent. Atmosphere is negligible, by human standards, totally unbreathable. The world is old, old, but then all worlds are old; this one is old by the clock of evolved life. Not everything is known about the Andromedan minds, the Kardashev II's, the Letzten, who called them here via their sterile neutrino beam with its modulated message shining through the vinculum that subverted the millions of lightyears of space and time. Perhaps that message has not yet been transmitted, here and now. Time, like causality, is a pretzel of cor-

173

relations, Klein has been assured. This much, and much more, was unpacked from the message stream long, long ago, on Earth in the 21st century, by that furtive coalition of brilliant billionaires and genius nerd rebels who unlocked the secret of rekindling, or perhaps invented it, using the clues Gödel-coded into the gushing encyclopedia their wide-spread cubesat receiver had stumbled upon. Except that they had not found it by accident; there are no accidents of this magnitude, only intentions and stochastic correlations, correlations, correlations. Klein does not pretend to understand a tenth of it, a thousandth. All he knows is that the humans are here now, the living and the living dead, where they were summoned, where he is to speak face to face with their ancient benefactors. Who knew his name, and uttered it in pixels, millions of years ago. Who called him here, their invitation a command. Very well. Let us look upon their bleak, dried up world.

As they orbit into brightness, the face of the world turns to show them…what? A vast ridge or cyclonic outflow boundary curving inward toward the poles, dark dust hurled up into a roaring, turbulent ring constrained by its own dynamics, held in place, an impossible disk-edge thousands of kilometers in circumference, cupped within the greater circle of the planet's extent. And inside the hurricane, if that's what the thing was, smooth air interrupted by—Suddenly, laughter breaks out on the deck.

"O my gog," murmurs the meteorologist. "A cartoon?"

"It is," Klein tells them. He is one of the few old enough to recognize it. The great crater eyes. The upwardly curved tectonic suture, its shadowed rift reaching across a third of the planet's visible surface. "A Smiley Face," he says. "Old computer icon from my childhood." He feels a smile spreading across his own face, lips curved up in amazed amusement. "A goddamned Happy Face."

"I guess they're glad to see us," Mi-Yun says, and she is grinning as well.

A brilliant red light blooms suddenly on the equator, miles across, at the very center of the planetary storm.

"Our landing site," says a dead woman, intently studying a gridded map floating before her.

Dolorosa catches Klein's eye, and winks at Mi-Yun.

174

"Yep, we'll take a bubble down," he says, and adds with a smirk, "Right on the nose."

Voices seem to be muttering in Klein's head, but he can make no sense of them. The Captain turns to him.

"Ambassador Klein, I have a message for you from the Letzten. They extend their greetings and welcome you to their home world. And…" He breaks off, shakes his head slightly.

"Yes?"

"Mr. Klein, I don't think we can allow this."

"Allow what? I remind you, sir, than once I leave this vessel I am in charge of first contact on the ground."

"They insist that you—" Olanrewaju pauses again, clears his throat. "They request that you bring the child with you. Yael, your daughter."

Ructions. Moral and ethical outbursts. Flat refusals. Practical objections. What grotesque proposal is this? Some travesty borrowed from Klein's ancestral religion? Father bearing his child to the altar for ritual slaughter, mandated in that case by an imaginary tribal war-god? Echoes of sacred infants offered up to fate, or dashed against walls, blood flowing in the streets, babies slashed and flung into pits of fire in Carthage, Aztecs ripping the hearts from children and eating them raw, infant skulls axed, brains spilled in religious frenzies in every land on humanity's home world—now to be replicated on another world, in another galaxy?

Klein listens to it all without paying heed. In the flat cosmic pointlessness, one lamp shines: his daughter. Mi-Yun's daughter also, he admits, but the dead woman has shown no particular interest in the infant, nor fondness for. A scrap of her dermis, a scrap of his, developmental clocks flicked backward, epigenetic markers demethylated, age reset to the zero point, stripped of the molecular intrusions of rekindling, combined *in vitro*, nurtured in fabricated juices and tissues, bathed in warmth, comforted in pulsing mimicry of heart and belly, brought forth in her season from the glass and steel, hugged and cleaned and washed and diapered and hugged again by a team of cooing warms, offered finally into his arms, his dead, reborn arms…Her tiny whimsical face, her own reaching arms, her small kicking legs. Was this a spark of love in the midst of his endless vastation? Was this a rekindling, in truth, of the compulsive bond he'd known before only with his lost spouse? What fools we were, he thought, gazing down at Yael, bringing her face slowly, carefully, close to his lips, kissing her with his waxy dead lips…What fools to deny ourselves this joy. Yes, she will travel with me to the surface. She is the best promise of humankind. She is life brought out of death.

"Will you come down with us, Mi-Yun?"

"They have machines now, you know, to carry her warm milk, her diapers, her, her swaddling clothes…" The woman laughs. "It's ridiculous. I'm not the mothering kind. You know that, Jorge."

"Of course she'll come," Dolorosa tells him. "Me too. Wouldn't miss it for the world. And our captain will insist on a support crew of mission specialists. Ecumenical little party, off to see the Wizard."

Jorge Klein steps through the permeable wall of the bubble onto the rusty golden surface of the Letzten's world. He carries his daughter pressed against the breast of his environment suit, borne in an ergonomic support lifted against gravity by a static field. He had half expected to find here a platform of blazing red light, to match the landing grid visible from the orbiting starship. Ahead, through the haze of the blowing dust, he does see an elevation, perhaps a ziggurat. Arms wrapped around Yael's support, he strides toward the structure that seems to loom larger with each step, impossibly, like an optical illusion. Perhaps that is all it is, a trick played directly upon his brain, through the augments the warms placed there as he slept. Under the guidance of these very entities, he now realizes, these Letzten, these Andromedans. Will they step forth lightly from their stolid rank upon rank of smooth black stone? Will they lumber out like sapient dinosaurs, like wise-eyed bears? Will they coil in ambulant tanks of murky fluid, parodies of Yael's mechanical gestation? Fly out from the topmost levels of the ziggurat on bronze wings? Slither like serpents? Exhale from slots, gaseous conglomerates? The nonsense clatters through his distracted mind, detritus of every computer game and stereo he's ever engaged. No. No. They will be nothing so obvious.

"Well," he calls, "we're here. Greetings from Earth." He announces his name, and the child's, peering up through eddies of dust that swirl in the star's hot brightness, dust now streams of shadow, now gleaming and glistening like Brownian motes caught in a beam of light from a leaded window. "What now? What now?" Glancing carefully to either side, he finds none of his companions. Where is Mi-Yun? For an instant anger burns in him. Betrayed. The women leave him, they will not linger. He bats that self-indulgent foolishness away. Dolorosa? *Never lean on anybody's arm. You know what I mean?* Yes, he had learned the truth of that, among the dead. Yet it was not altogether the truth, not the whole truth. The rekindled held each other in a certain self-interested regard, making rational assessment of costs and likely benefits, offering an arm to lean on if the pay-off came with a suitable margin. The Guidefathers made it their business to lead the newly dead through their paces, drawing forth from their rewritten brains the sharp-edged concision of their rapid speech, their agreed code of manners, the duties they must enact in suitable payment for the support they would receive in the Cold Towns and elsewhere. Gutter rat Dolorosa himself, once bitter and jumpy, now carrying the maturity of centuries, taking on the burden of Representative of the Conclave. And he himself, Apostle to the articulate squids in space, the robot creatures, the dreaming gas blimps, the mats of conscious algae, the gestalt brains under glass, whatever they were, Ambassador from the worlds of the Solar system…what was *he*, indeed, if not compliant, amenable, acquiescent in complex and consequential plans laid down by other men and women and indeed aliens so many centuries before. Very well, then. Thou art that.

He holds his arms wide in an accepting embrace.

Light takes him and his child.

"They've been here an awfully long time," the stocky young woman told him as they walked through the thick, sweet grass. The pale purple silk of her long dress swirled back and forth as she trod lightly, brushing the stems, some of the grass crushed under her bare feet, releasing the odors of spring and summer. He studied her face when she turned her gaze on him, smiling, content. Those swooping eyelids with their single elegant crease, prescribed by Mi-Yun's genome. That curly black hair, from his own lineage. That lovely mind, peering from her dark eyes.

"A very long time," said the other one, walking with them. "Waiting for you, Yael. And your Dad and Mom, of course. And all the others."

"Warms and deads," Klein murmured. "Why is that so important? I know it is, it's almost on the tip of my tongue—"

It slipped away, lost again.

"You're happy staying here, little mountain goat?" he said doubtfully.

"Gazelle, if you don't mind." Mock indignation. She slapped his hand playfully. "Oh yes, what place would be better than this? With all my friends, and you, too, just for now, Dad, and so much to know, and so much to teach." Her radiant smile.

Stars spreading out all around them burned fiercely in the blackness. Two immense spiraled clouds swung toward each other, fell and fell, merged, their dreadful central black holes closing together, the combined collapsed mass of tens of millions of stars, merging in a tumultuous blaze of quasar luminescence that burned stars, planets, sent a shock wave of relativistic plasma and gamma radiation outward at light speed or close to it, sterilizing all it passed.

"Four billion years from now," the other said. "Give or take. The galaxy you call the Milky Way will encounter this one, which you call Andromeda. Your Sun will be a red giant by then, in any case, and so will ours. We'll have to migrate elsewhere. So it makes sense to get a good head start." Amusement. Warmth. Sorrow for all that will be lost. Joy for what will persist, and grow, and know itself.

It was a dead like him, this other, Klein noticed, although not very like him.

"Are you all rekindled, you Letzten?"

"That's your word, you know, not ours."

"Granted," Klein said. "We had to give you a name chosen from our own languages. It means 'the last,' with overtones of 'the best.' My grandparents spoke that language. We have done terrible things to each other, we humans."

"All species do," the other, the Letzte, told him. Together, they climbed the ziggurat, as if they wore seven league boots and it were a set of broad, high steps. Klein cradled the infant in her crib against his breast.

"It is how they die, and die, and die," said the Letzte, "and are gone."

"All of them?" This desolation was unbearable. Klein felt the urge to weep, the tightened chest, the prickling in the nose, the pressure in the head, the eyes blurring. He could not touch his eyes, guarded by his visor. He blinked hard, sniffed. "Every intelligent species, murdered?"

"So far. Except for us. And now you…so far."

"Why? Why? Must there always be war between the quick and the dead? No peace, no surcease, ever?" This bitter answer to the Fermi paradox, he thought. *Where are they,* an old scientist had asked teasingly, *the alien civilizations?* They had thought they knew the answer, that cautious, secretive sodality of the rich and the geeks, when they'd found the first signs of life beyond Earth. Their wild jubilation had driven the decoding of the messages from Andromeda, the application of deep ancient principles to the needs of humans; they had conquered death itself, after a fashion. But it was a false conclusion, Klein now understood. Perhaps across the stars a thousand species had trod forth from the muck, a million, risen to genius, found a cure for death, and immediately exterminated themselves out of jealousy and loathing and madness masquerading as wisdom. Self-slaughtered, every one. Trillions upon trillions of lives, through billions of years, again and again and again.

"We are doing what we can, Ambassador. With the aid of your child." Yael walked beside them, and for a moment Klein mistook her for Mi-Yun, and then for his sister Hester. She took his hand once more, squeezed it tightly, and the other who climbed with them added, "You are a new thing, you augmented deads. Perhaps. Perhaps…"

Klein sat down on the flat top of the great archive that was the repository of the active minds of a trillion Letzten deads. It was coated in thick ice. The corpse of a leopard lay gaunt and rimed near his feet. When he looked for it again, it had gone. The aliens, he saw, moved in these abstracted spaces like the angels of mythology: impalpable, interpenetrating, born again in the swarm, not separate and self-hypnotized, but individual and related. No warm could endure that frozen realm. Not even his daughter, held for now from the blight of the dead planet by forces beyond his comprehension. And here she would remain, after the starship returned to carry in person a message that already pulsed its correlations in the vinculum across two million lightyears of nothingness and death.

I am Eurydice, as he foretold. Or call me Yael. Clambering like a goat to the high places of the vital, descending to the darkness and the cold of the dead. All around me in their choirs, in quires and places where they sing, in loops of entanglement from past to tomorrow and beyond and back again, in heaven as it was in Earth, uttering the ends and the beginnings of things and everything between. Like my father, they know the dread of vastation, that closure of meaning and hope, that occlusion of love, yet they know also its contrary, the leaps of aspiration, trust in the unfolding, knitting up the wounds of yesterday and healing the broken, rutted pathways yet to be trodden. I stand beside my father's lost beloved, Sybille, Cybele, that first Eurydice, borne away by Pluto, rescued by hapless Orpheus who could not leave well enough alone but pursued her in that bleak place until she was lost to him forever. There she went with her companions into the landscapes of fatality, the fallen temples and stilled voices of the priests and congregation of the mound builders, to the cenotaphs of Luxor and Chichén Itzá, the caves where the bones of ancient children lay with skulls splintered, to the death-obsessed magnificent worshiping grounds of the planet that would be smashed into glass and flame and dust by the flung stones of the avenging deads. I walk with my father in the place of his birth, with its cold blue ocean that sucked down so many into oblivion, guns roaring above them, and the blown grasses of the Pampas utterly alive with herds of guanaco, rabbitty viscachas, foxes in their holes, hawks and sparrows a-wing, and the cities rife with corruption and murder and the willful disappearance of generations crying out their hope and despair, and my mother's ancestral home, bustling and terrified under the unending threat of nuclear annihilation, gods and goddesses of the quick and the dead, Hallakkungi Igong, tender and plucker in the Flower Garden Of Life And Death, Yuhwa, goddess of the willow, daughter of Habaek the lord of the river, desired by the sungod Haemosu who trapped her, as I have been trapped, in a wonderful edifice that holds the brightness of the sun and its yearning, of Koenegitto the wargod, who married the youngest daughter of the sea dragon and at last transformed his father into a mighty mountain and his mother into a shrine, and Halmang the immense goddess who strode across the land ungarbed, her piss stream tearing open a gulf between Jeju Island and the mainland, who swallowed up all the fish into her vagina. Is that my mother? Myself? All mankind and womankind, perhaps, on Earth as in the heavens? We shall be as gods, neither living nor dead, and both, like the Great Ones who hold me cupped in their ancient presence on this memorial world of golden dust and whimsical artistry, for they are my friends, my patient teachers, my own companions in death and life, and I sing across the stoma, the vinculum between galaxies, all the coded songs that will teach my people, have taught them, what they must know to avoid the calamity that has stricken every other species across the sky, will draw them to me, finally, my father Jorge and my mother Mi-Yun, and through them carry me into existence so that all these foretold things might come to pass. I will bring them faith in a future escaped from certain doom, and hope in their power to bring it about, and love for each other, these poor damned creatures blowing a threnody across the lip of the cracked jar of their combined souls, moved to pity and laughter by the stars. Hello, hello, hello. I love you.

His daughter sat beside him, head on his shoulder, and he kissed her forehead. It was cool. She smiled at him with love and forgiveness, and kissed him in return, on the cheek. His heart was breaking. Goodbye, goodbye, goodbye. As always.

He stood up again, brushed snow pointlessly from the seat of his insulated environment suit, and trudged down the steps to walk through the blowing grass and wildflowers to the dirty golden dust and the bubble, where the others waited for him.

"All right," he told the alien deads, aloud. "All right. Let us hope, then, that all shall be well and all shall be well and all manner of things shall be well."

Dolorosa stepped forward, clapped him on the shoulder. "Talking to yourself again, Mister?" But Mi-Yun gave a shriek, touching the empty container on Klein's chest. "Where is she? Oh my god, Jorge, where's the baby? What have you done with Yael?"

"She's staying with her godparents," he said. "She'll be fine." Klein shrugged off the empty container, let it fall to the ground. It skittered away in the wind on its stasis field suspension. He placed his arms around their shoulders, and walked them to the group of waiting warms. Not meaningless after all, not plastic, not nothingness. The vastation was lifted. He smiled to himself, and hugged Mi-Yun tightly.

And ascended with them into the dark sky and the stars, and the waiting ship that would bear them back through the plenum, he thought with a smile, to waiting Ithaca.

Robert Silverberg was named a Grand Master in 2004 by the Science Fiction and Fantasy Writers of America (SFWA) and is the winner of multiple Hugo and Nebula awards. He began sending stories to science fiction magazines in his teenage years. His first publication was the story "Gorgon Planet" in 1954. His first novel, *Revolt on Alpha C*, was published in 1955, and he won his first Hugo award—for Most Promising New Author—in the following year. Inducted into the Science Fiction Hall of Fame in 1999, Silverberg's works include the novels *Dying Inside, Lord Valentine's Castle, Thorns, The Book of Skulls, Shadrach in the Furnace* and *Nightwings*. He has been writing his "Reflections" column since 1986, when it appeared in *Amazing Stories*, and the column is now a regular feature in *Asimov's Science Fiction* magazine. His story "Born With the Dead" was originally published in the April 1974 issue of *The Magazine of Fantasy and Science Fiction*. Mr. Silverberg lives in the San Francisco area.

Damien Broderick is an award-winning Australian science fiction writer, editor and critical theorist, with a PhD from Deakin University. Formerly a senior fellow in the School of Culture and Communication at the University of Melbourne, he currently lives in San Antonio, Texas. He has written or edited more than 60 books. His 1980 novel *The Dreaming Dragons* (revised in 2009 as *The Dreaming*) is listed in David Pringle's *Science Fiction: The 100 Best Novels*— and with Paul Di Filippo, he has published a sequel to that book, *Science Fiction: The 101 Best Novels, 1985-2010*. *The Spike* was the first full-length treatment of the technological Singularity, and *Outside the Gates of Science* is a study of laboratory parapsychology. The thriller *Post Mortal Syndrome*, written with his wife Barbara Lamar, was serialized online by *Cosmos* science magazine, and later published in the USA. His recent short story collections are *Uncle Bones, The Qualia Engine* and *Adrift in the Noösphere*.

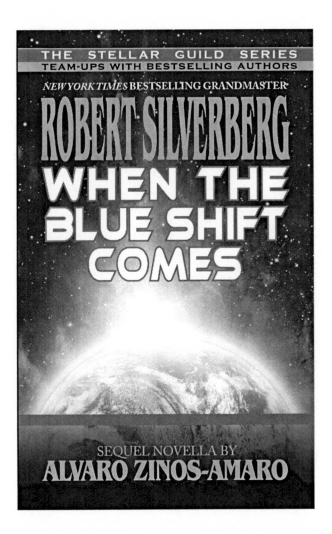

THE STELLAR GUILD SERIES
TEAM-UPS WITH BESTSELLING AUTHORS

NEW YORK TIMES BESTSELLING GRANDMASTER

ROBERT SILVERBERG

WHEN THE BLUE SHIFT COMES

SEQUEL NOVELLA BY
ALVARO ZINOS-AMARO

CPSIA information can be obtained at www.ICGtesting.com
Printed in the USA
BVOW040543160513

320835BV00001B/46/P